A Bad Afternoon for a Piece of Cake

A Collection of Ten Short Stories

by

Diane Ladd

EXXCELL
PRESS

This first edition published by

Inkwell Productions, Scottsdale Arizona

in conjunction with Exxcell Press, Ojai, California

Printed and Formatted in the United States of America

ISBN: 978-0-9-883568-9-4

Library of Congress Control Number: 2012923211

Published by Inkwell Productions
10869 N. Scottsdale Road # 103-128
Scottsdale, AZ 85254-5280

Tel. 480-315-3781
E-mail info@inkwellproductions.com
Website www.inkwellproductions.com

Printed in the United States of America

Novelist STEPHAN KANFER lauds Diane Ladd

It's no news that Diane Ladd is one of the greatest actresses in the history of American cinema, phenomenally adept at comedy and tragedy. What is news is that she now demonstrates an equal mastery of the short story form. In *A Bad Afternoon for a Piece of Cake* Ladd shows us a pitch-perfect ear for regional as well as urban dialogue, an innate wit, and a sure hand at plotting and narrative. Perhaps this is less of a surprise than it first appears—she is, after all, a cousin of Tennessee Williams.

– STEFAN KANFER, author

Groucho, Ball of Fire, Somebody, Tough Without a Gun, Ball of Fire and other Bestsellers

Author, Critic REX REED praises Diane Ladd

Southern writers have a unique talent for feel, touch, smell, and taste that doesn't seem to exist anywhere else. Truman Capote had this extraordinary gift. So did Flannery O'Connor, Eudora Welty, Carson McCullers, and Tennessee Williams among others. They felt the snow, smelled the honeysuckle, heard the wind through the loblolly pines, tasted the sweet tea. And they got it down on paper with a wrenching sensitivity that turned into literature.

Diane Ladd has it, too—as an actress, as a humanitarian, and as a writer of prose that makes cracker barrel talk as down-home unpretentious as a buttermilk biscuit suddenly sound downright patrician. The characters in these stories laugh, cry, bleed and leave behind a legacy not easily forgotten. They come from Mississippi towns called Meridian, Poplarville, and Tupelo, and end up in cities called Chicago, San Francisco, and Manhattan, but no matter how they learn or lose or love, they never cease to cherish a Porsche 911 GT2 or a cold bottle of Orange Crush with equal relish. Diane Ladd is one of them. From the Mississippi Delta to Broadway and Hollywood, she has forgotten nothing and retained everything.

What a thrill to read what she knows in the words of characters as rich and colorful as fields of sunflowers: a man whose homophobia backfires because he's wearing an orange jacket, a garden that flourishes from the bodies of mercury-poisoned miners in the cemetery underneath, a statuesque mulatto on her first day at Juilliard. You can't learn this stuff in a writing class. You absorb the stories you hear, hold them close, stamp them in your memory. Then on a bad afternoon for a piece of cake, you write them down and tell them to the world, the way they were told to you. And you become a Southern writer, on your way to a new adventure. How blessed we are to share this one with Diane Ladd.

– REX REED, author and renowned critic
Valentines & Vitriol, People are Crazy Here, Personal Effects and other Bestsellers

What is straight?

A line can be straight, or a street,

but the human heart, oh, no,

it's curved like a road through mountains.

Tennessee Williams

A Bad Afternoon for a Piece of Cake

Most people are so busy picking up rhinestones,

trying to get rich, they don't see the

Diamonds life sends them . . .

Acknowledgements

My special thanks to my beloved husband, Robert C. Hunter and my beautiful daughter, Laura Dern for their love and constant encouragement.

A special Thanks to my editor, Karen Price-Mueller and to Nick Ligidakas for his passion to publish this book.

My Mentors: the late great Paddy Chayefsky and my cousin, Tennessee Williams for their belief in me and and to my fellow Mississippian writers; the late Willie Morris; Eudora Welty and Flannery O'Connor for their inspiration.

To the Exxcell Entertainment staff and loyal assisstants: Brittany Bolduc, Stephanie Bullock, Sylvia Hague, and Bonnie White who always help take care of business while I hide out and take time for myself to write! My fabulous Press Reps., New York's Richard Rubenstein; and California's Lori Jonas for their support. My Staunch New York playwright's and musical lawyers, Jason Baruch and Jason Aylesworth, as well as my Bebverly Hills Attorney Fred Toczek, who apply their legal expertise with integrity.

And to my business manager, Amir Malek, whose business proficiency soothes my foundation.

TABLE OF CONTENTS

Tadpole Tag

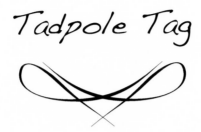

Mary stepped out of the drug store, tucking the newspaper under her arm, carefully cradling the two bags of rationed coffee. She turned to wave at the now alone elderly clerk and suddenly saw stars as she spun and stumbled.

While her packages flew, she grabbed at the piney mailbox to keep from going to her knees. She hadn't seen the boys – three of 'em – as they bolted around the corner like lightning, out of the blue.

"Cheeze!" the sandy-haired one yelled at his friends. "What's the matter with you, boy? You almost knocked over a pregnant lady! Where was you born, in a barn?"

"Ah, man, haven't you heard? He wasn't born – he was shot out on a whorehouse wall and hatched by the sun!" the third boy yelled back, not missing a step as he laughed, following his fleeing leader.

"Are you all right, ma'am?" said the sandy-haired boy. He was blushing.

"Yes, I am. I think so." She knew the other one had said something dirty – or so she thought – but didn't know what he meant.

The boy stooped quickly to hide his embarrassment and gathered up her packages. Hesitantly, he extended them to her.

"We was playing tadpole tag. Gee, I'm awfully sorry… we…" He looked down at his feet and as he scuffed one against the other.

"Thank you, young man," she said, absolving him from his burden. "It's real sweet of you to be so concerned, but I'm just fine. You run on now."

Turning, he hastily scurried away, following the others.

Taking a deep breath, Mary moved her hands down the form that served as the protective sky of her future child's hidden universe. This form, her flesh, her stomach. Stillness!

"Why aren't you moving?" she whispered. Just didn't seem natural, her being so upset and her own flesh and blood staying so quiet. "Well, my dear one, if you're calm, I guess everything's all right."

Readjusting her paper and parcels she started down the street toward home. The gentle but determined young woman stretched to her full five feet, two inches and hooded her eyes as she looked skyward. The sun's still yellow rays reflected against the dull metal of the tall ole water tank, the town's landmark.

"Must be about 5:30," she thought. "Where is Percy?"

Tossing her long blond hair back off her high cheek-boned face, she savored the late afternoon breeze brushing across her porcelain skin. She listened to her own footsteps crunching in the gravel as she walked on. She nodded to a passing lady, wondering who she was. She thought she knew nearly 'bout everybody in town, even though she'd only been here a short time.

"Such a beautiful day!" she said to herself. "Doesn't seem possible to be so late in November. Seems like God always gives you pretty weather for a holiday."

She had to turn sideways so she could see the step onto the sidewalk. Sometimes she thought she must be having twins but, the doctor said no. "Positively only one."

"A boy," she mused. She just felt it was going to be a son. "What will he be like? Will he be like those boys? If so, which one? The leader, running on? The middle one, making dirty remarks and sneering like a fool? Or the last, considerate? Is it how you bring 'em up?"

She turned in toward the house. Their landlady, Mrs. Combs, opened the screen door for her.

"Hello, Mrs. Taylor, back so soon?"

"Yes, I'm 'fraid so." Mary smiled at the woman, who reminded her of the grandmother everyone wanted.

"Well, that walk did you good. You look mighty pretty. But your face is all flushed." She put the back of her knowing hand against Mary's forehead. "Why, child, you feel a mite warm, ain't getting a cold, are you?"

"No, ma'am," Mary replied, even though she did feel out of sorts.

"I want you to take good care of yourself. You let me know, now, if you don't feel right any time. Oh, and by the way, a young girl, one of yoah husband's relatives, stopped by."

"Which one?" she asked. Percy had so many.

"That little girl, J. Honey Bea. Said she rode in town with her Daddy and wanted to know if you'd play some jacks with her."

"That's Preston's little sister," Mary laughed. "Maybe it's a good thing I wasn't here. We played last week and I couldn't get up off the floor afterward. Oh, and Mrs. Combs, here's a present. Coffee – a bag of special blend coffee. You've been so dear to Percy and me."

"My goodness," Mrs. Combs fluttered with embarrassment, being one of those good souls to whom it comes easy to give but who hasn't ever learned how to comfortably receive. "You shouldn't do this, but thank you so much. Mrs. Taylor. Do you expect Mr. Taylor in this evening?"

"Not sure, really. I guess. Depends how much work he has left and how far away he is."

Taking in the melancholy look in Mary's eyes, Mrs. Combs sat down on the porch swing and folded her hands. She smiled slowly, the folds of her cheeks lifting, removing the marks of time. A little girl now asking her best friend, "Well, I guess y'all be going ovah to his family's for Thanksgiving dinner tomorrow but if he should get delayed for any reason," Mrs. Combs cleared her throat. "I mean, I thought if possibly if he wasn't coming in, you'd join me for dinner. Fixed something special for the holiday. Chick'n n' dumplin's, with cranberries, creamed corn, black eyed peas n' okra. And I've got a banana cream pie! And some of my own iced tea!" Stopping the swing, she sighed, stood up, and moved over to a small table with assorted plants on it.

"Thank you. I'm going to freshen up." Turning before the smile could leave her face, Mary went down the high-ceilinged hall of the old house and into their bedroom. She knew Mrs. Combs was not expecting her own son and had indeed gone to all that trouble just for Mary. Crossing to the huge four-poster mahogany bed, she turned back the white chenille bedspread, and on a second thought, also turned down the soft feather quilt. After all, if Mrs. Combs was good enough to let her use nice things, she could certainly take good care of 'em.

Easing herself into a sitting position and folding her hands in her lap, she felt the taut muscles in her face relax. All her personal belongings were in Mobile, in trunks. Her thoughts moved to Percy. "Uh, I'd better stop calling him that!" Mary thought. His name *had been* Percy Paul Williams. He related with pride that when he was fourteen he'd earned that three dollars *especially*, 'cause that's what it cost. Said he chopped wood for Farmer Miller, next door, until he had blisters big as quarters on his hands. He went directly to the Judge where they held court in the back room of the general store. Then he'd become Preston Paul Williams, never more to wake to the embarrassing yell of "Percyyyy!"

But from the day Preston told her the story, she couldn't disassociate him from being Percy. It was like him – obstinate, charming, corny, compelling, as well as unforgettable. Mary loved words. She loved to rhyme them, sing them and see how many could explain a person or place. Preston thought it was a silly game. She didn't know if that was because he left school after the sixth grade and didn't want to be found out. He had told her himself, with his head back and his chin firm, proud. But he didn't like for her to bring it up.

Unfolding her soft, graceful hands and touching the patterns in the quilt, her eyes examined the careful stitches along the beautiful blue and gold designs. Preston had assured her they'd only be here for a couple of weeks. He just had to have his family meet his bride. They'd been married just eleven months ago. Even though she was with child and would rather have waited, she'd agreed. A couple of weeks had turned into five months.

There in the Magnolia land of Southern Mississippi lived Preston's parents, four of his six sisters, one of his three brothers and all of their families, interlaced throughout a sixteen-mile area. The ambiance of the country was soothing. Aside from the taboo of poverty's pain, one wouldn't even know that it was wartime. The river flowed with the memory of all who'd passed through Pearl River County: Indians, Spanish, French, British – explorers, settlers, slaves, missionaries, and the pioneers. Many who'd worked and planted – they ultimately enjoyed, times good and bad.

Situated here, Preston figured, they'd see all his relatives sooner or later. They rented from Mrs. Combs' boarding house: two rooms – a bedroom and a kitchen. Mary had wanted a larger apartment, especially a room to fix up for the baby, but Preston said they couldn't afford it. "Besides, we won't be staying long. Ah don't like putting money in somebody else's pocket. I won't mind paying high interest on our own home someday, but in the meantime, ain't gonna make somebody else rich. Nah, Sir!"

Mary looked at her little gold wrist watch. Everybody – cousins, uncles, aunts and friends – would be gathered at his folks' home to celebrate the Thanksgiving supper. Preston was off selling his chicken medicine. He'd said, "Baby, if I'm far away and doing good, not going to stop, rush back and let any 'ole damn holiday cost us money."

By now, Preston was probably putting plenty of miles on that 1936 Ford he'd just bought. Only six years old, ran like new, and he'd only paid $89 for it. He'd wanted that new Chevrolet with open cab and pickup box but it cost a ridiculous $440. Beloved humorist Will Rogers, who'd been killed in a plane crash in Alaska, rocking all of America, said, "America was the only nation in the history of the world to go to the poor house in an automobile." Mary was glad Preston bought the Ford 'cause she sure didn't want to be bounced around in any ole pick-up.

Meanwhile, down in the sweltering Delta that Thanksgiving Day, folks mourned all over the county for one of their own, Bubba Boy Johnson, only nineteen, who had been blown to pieces. Not in the war effort. He'd been classified as 4F, either as "flat-footed" or "queer," as town folk gossiped. Bubba was neither, but his cousin, an important doctor, had lied good for him so he wouldn't have to serve. Even though bad Bubba was a coward, folks loved 'im and mourned him anyhow. His demise hadn't anything to do with the times, only his own. Bubba had been siphoning gas out of an oil truck, stealing yet again, when the ashes of his cigarette fell into a gas puddle right underneath the tank.

Although they were mourning Bubba along with everybody else, the Taylor family was listening to the news of other travesties, talk of those guys, Hirohito and Mussolini – "Mew Salami," as J. Honey Bea called him – but hell, they weren't even sure where Ethiopia was. Couldn't pay no mind to the news anyway 'cause they were worried about getting a good dinner on the table. Gonna be 'bout 25 relatives coming over, maybe 38, if some of the dog kin were feeling broke or lonely.

Hattie, Preston's momma, wondered, "How can I get somebody else besides J.J. to bless the food? Older he gets, more spiritual he gets, longer the blessings get!" Only last month he'd taken to including reading a couple of chapters of the Bible as part of the grace until Aunt Tessie, famished, almost passed out. Truth was Preston's daddy J.J. was an 'ole hellcat! No getting around it.

Like when they were first married. J.J. didn't much like Hattie's coffee. One day he just stood up from the table, grabbed up the pot and his gun, stomped to the back screen door, threw it open, hurled the pot high in the air, and blew it to smithereens.

Of course Hattie, all 5 foot nothin' of 'er, had set demarcation lines as well. When pregnant with her first child, she'd gotten a phone call from a so-called well-meaning neighbor.

"You're being done wrong, dear one!" the neighbor said. "Yoah husband J.J. is running around with a school teacher and they are meeting up this very night."

Now Hattie, pregnant and all, got in the buckboard and went to the supposed tryst spot. There she found his horse and another strange horse tied to the fence alongside that gravel road. Softly, she treaded 'cross leaves, brush, and woods through the dark night. Sounds of heavy breathing, moans and two people getting it on led her way.

A startled J.J. looked up into the blinding beam of a flashlight. All he heard was one word which floated from his own wife's voice. "FINISH!"

"What the?" he exclaimed.

Behind the beam, Hattie repeated herself with more conviction, "I *said*, finish!" accompanied by the metallic slide of her gun's bolt.

Either J.J. was a hell of a man, or the greatest faker of them all, but he finished with a great sigh.

Hattie said, "Get up." He complied.

"Now, sir, zip up THAT fly," which he did.

Then she turned on the nearly apoplectic "lady" who stood, brushing the leaves off her long skirt. "Miss, you weren't forewarned before but now you are. This is MY man and if I *EVER* catch you with him again, honey... Well, I'm a God-fearing woman, but it just might be in me to blow your head off, leave it on a stump, walk away blessing you, and never look back! So, stay out of my sight." The woman appropriately scurried off.

The two of them alone, she turned to her husband. "Now, sir, you started something else you're going to by-God finish – a marriage and a family!" Without another word, she turned and stomped away.

His horse tied to the buckboard, he talked to her on the way home only to be met with her stern silence in return. Later, she played the piano, filling the air with music, drowning any of his possible lies. The amazing thing, if you think about it, is that she never brought it up again. Not once.

Many assumed J.J., who was a rounder, did cheat. Thing is, if so, he never again got caught. Now he'd taken to reading the Bible and giving everybody righteous advice.

Never did anyone think of crossing Hattie, and when she said something, people jumped. Just now, she had a dinner to cook.

"Aileen," she called to her tall daughter, who was daydreaming as usual, with visions, God knows, Hattie couldn't understand. "C'mon, Aileen... if we wait for you, the dog'll die before dinner's served."

Hattie laughed to herself, thinking she could utter all the nonsense she wanted, 'cause nobody paid an ounce of attention to what she said anyhow. Only two of her many children understood her sense of humor: Preston, (God, she hoped he'd show up today,) and J. Honey Bea, her youngest, who was also driving her crazy. Most of the time, even though she loved them, trying to talk to her own family felt like swimming through an underwater-barrier.

Aileen looked at her mother from far off in another dimension. "Why can't I just say to my own mother, I *hate* whipping the damn mashed 'taters!" she muttered to herself. But God forbid Aileen should utter a curse word. Her mama would slap her but good! She stared at the white blob in the bowl. Could it've only been last week? God, she loved her boyfriend so much. He was going to ask her to be his wife. She knew it. And she was gonna love that man forever and ever. But, God, he might not even show up today. Aileen wiped away a tear, remembering. They'd all been sitting down to the table so nice, just about to break bread, when J. Honey Bea had opened that rotten little mouth of hers.

"Mama, what's saltpeter?" Aileen had just about died.

The night before, her daddy'd said to Mama, "By God, no daughter of mine's gonna date a man in the military without us putting saltpeter in his food."

Tried in vain, Mama did try to change the subject, but J. Honey Bea kept ON with a wicked little grin, "But, Mama is it good? I heard Daddy tell you tonight to put it in the mashed potatoes!"

Everybody had just sat there silently staring at the white blobs on their plates. The embarrassment of the memory made Aileen sick.

Just as she got up her courage to object to her task, Hattie suddenly marched away and switched off the radio. J.J. sat up with a start, newspaper dropping from his lap. "What the…"

"I've had enough noise of news!" Hattie shook her head with exasperation.

"Goddamn, woman, I don't care about the son-of-a-bitch war. I'm waiting to hear 'bout the Goddamn labor disputes!"

"J.J. Taylor, will you please watch your mouth, sir? Stop that cursing. Preston's coming and he's bringing Mary, and you remember she's Catholic. She doesn't want to hear any cussing, thank you."

"Catholic, ahh sweet Jesus," J.J. moaned mockingly. "Don't remind me." Then he chuckled and whispered mischievously to J. Honey Bea, "You know what the Catholics do, don't you? Their priests catch you at night and tote you in a croaker sack to the devil!" He smacked his lips as if he believed it.

"Oh, J.J!" Hattie exclaimed angrily. "You stop those lies. It's you who's going to hell, sir, and you won't need anybody to tote you there!"

J.J. jumped to his feet. "Madam, you are just angry because your dumplings are too tough again. I tasted 'em. I can't do anything about that. And you're also angry because your youngest here spent her whole allowance on that ridiculous low-cut angora sweater."

"Gawd," J. Honey Bea cried, "It only shows my collar bone!"

Meanwhile, one Preston Paul Taylor, driving down that Oxford, Mississippi highway in his new-to-him, second-hand, fancy Ford, was looking for houses with chickens. He was selling his medicine for poultry, livestock, and the immediate cure of cholera, roup, sour head, white diarrhea, removal of worms, parasites, and increased egg production. Not being able to find any music, he switched off the radio. Wasn't interested in listening to some damn businessmen running off at the mouth about labor disputes. Sweet Jesus, President Roosevelt'd told the people, "Freedom requires *well defined licenses* in order to protect itself." Why, against protests, he'd even signed the National Labor Relations Act! That man had guts! Now, wouldn't you know that our own damn Supreme Court had gone and reversed the National Industrial Recovery Act. Caused uproar with organized labor, implying that any government attempt to legislate prices, wages and working conditions would be unconstitutional! Who could imagine that?

Preston shrugged helplessly and thought to himself, "Why the hell should I care? I'm my own boss. Even with all the damn gas rationing, I can, by-God, manage."

"Morning," Preston yelled out the window as his Ford pulled into the one-gasoline pump store. "Fill it up," he smiled, stepping out of the car, picking up a rag hanging off the side of the pump hose and, circling his prize possession, he sure enough spotted a scratch some damned piece of gravel had caused during his day's travels. Spitting on the rag, he began to polish. Mary taught him not to run out of gas, which he'd done on occasion, his mind being on singing songs and not paying attention to boring things like a fuel gauge. Suddenly, his attention was diverted. Out of the corner of his eye, he saw a bum moving off the road towards him. Preston shifted uncomfortably from one foot to the other.

The man, his head down, as if he wasn't worthy to look up at heaven, timidly but desperately put his hand out. "'Scuse me, sir, could you spare five cents for a cup of soup?"

"Hell, man," Preston replied sincerely before he could stop himself, "Where you gonna find soup for 5 cents?" Then they stood there quietly, the two men, seconds seeming like a lifetime. Maybe it was, in some strange way. "Listen," Preston murmured. "I'm not gonna give you money. How do I know you're not gonna buy booze? But, I'll buy you some lunch."

Putting the rag down, he went inside as the man followed him silently as a worn-out dog. Preston purchased two large hunks of cheese, two boxes of Saltine crackers and two Orange Crush drinks.

"Here," handing the man his share. "Same lunch as me. Not much, but it'll fill a hole in your stomach."

Taking two cigars out of his pocket, Preston noted then the surprised pleasure that danced over the man's tired face as he handed him one. Turning, he nodded to the two men in the corner, playing checkers, watching him.

Back on his route, Preston drove past the squalid railroad camps constructed from junk piles, improvised shelters made of remnants of boxes, cloths, and discarded cans and papers. Saw lean looks on disillusioned, trapped faces. Heard farmers discussing the fact that milk, in order to raise the sale price, was being poured out on the ground even though children were starving. And corn, which could have been eaten, was being burned for fuel in stoves to warm the body before it froze.

"Damn." Preston, frustrated, hit the steering wheel with his fist. "What a mess."

With one hand, his fingers unwrapped the cellophane from his cherished cigar while he remembered the words of Will Rogers. Maybe Rogers'd said it all, "What America needs is another orange juice drink for a nickel." Biting off the tip of the cigar, Preston spit it out, then instead of lighting it, bit off a big piece and began to chew, tucking the rest away for later. He drove on down the road.

It saddened Mary that Preston didn't feel he should be home with her to share Thanksgiving. She'd overheard one of the cousins snickering about Preston staying away a lot to play with his chickens – blonde, brunette, and red-heads. Mary's daddy had always said, "When somebody's talking like a fool, don't get down on their level 'cause then you're a fool, too!" So she'd just ignored that tacky little cousin.

She raised herself from the bed and crossed to the bureau. Suppose she hadn't met Preston. Well, then she would have married Joe – conservative, traditionally dependable Catholic Joe, her childhood romantic sweetheart. What a different world that would have been. But she'd met Preston, and she'd never known anybody like him. "Drop dead handsome," all the girls said, and that's what they were doing, flitting all around him like bees after honey, with his wavy black hair and twinkling black eyes, flashing a pearly white, devastating smile that charmed the petals right off the rose. Wearing that camel-hair overcoat, spats, and a fedora, and carrying a black walking stick, he'd strode right into Mary's life and never left. Isn't it odd how a turn around a corner can change your whole life? What was it they say?

One path leads to summer; one path leads to winter or fall.

One path leads to spring; and one path to something, or nothing at all.

Folding the lace dickey, she thought, "I'll save it for a rainy day," and closed the drawer. Straightening, she caught her reflection in the mirror. Only then did she realize that her eyes were filled with tears. Her own eyes, blue as light crystal, so different from his eyes - black as sin, they were called, those eyes she loved so much.

"This is ridiculous," she thought, brushing the tears away. "What on earth is the matter with me – this completely despondent mood?" She shook her finger at herself in the mirror, "All right now, Mary Elizabeth Wilson, you stop this!"

The little bouquet of daisies on top of the bureau caught her attention. Some had already died. The middle looked alive, but the leaves had fallen together like the flower had just stepped out of a swim. Maybe if she gave them some coffee grounds and an aspirin, it would help. Two of them were quite alive, like they had never been picked.

"Poor little flowers," she thought. "You were seeded, planted, nourished, grew, then picked and put in an old vase, and here you will finish out your life. And if I don't look at you and soak up your bright yellow, perfect formation, your life will be in vain. That's what life is like, most of the time. Result depends on some soul like me who'll pass you right by. But, I'll say thank you today and I'll give you water. Come on…"

Smiling, she brushed the petals of one of the fresher daisies against her cheek. She turned, and then, there it was! She stood motionless, waiting… for time. Her toes curled downward toward the floor. Either they wanted better balance or they wanted to get closer to the heart of the foot. Each second seemed like an eternity. The silence wasn't silent enough. She wanted to hear the sound of her feelings. Had it been her imagination? The palms of her hand grew damp and she pressed the vase even tighter. "Preston, please come."

No! There! It had not been her imagination. That sharp pain, different from any other. Her heart began to pound. "My God, I'm afraid."

She sat there looking at the clock, her fingers clenching and unclenching like little roly-poly balls. "I want my mother," she said aloud. As friendly or open as Preston's family was, sensing they might make fun of her, she'd been afraid to voice any fear. All so pioneerish. Why, only the other day, one of his sisters, Cora, told her about giving birth last month to Junior. Said she got up to call the doctor and halfway across the room had to stop - the head was coming out! Couldn't walk, so Cora lay right down on the floor and Junior just popped out. Preston's mother had given birth to twelve, all in her own home. Of course, they never talked about the fact that three of those children had died at birth. It was those three that Mary kept thinking of now.

Her own family seemed so far away. Had her mother been this alone when she gave birth to her first child? That, too, would have been for love. Her mother Rose was French-German and descended from gracious, elegant aristocracy, whose great wealth had been confiscated in Europe.

In fact, on their twenty-first birthdays, the two elder sisters, Mary's aunts, had each been given fifty percent ownership of a shipyard to teach them business sense. But her mother did not receive that famous twenty-first birthday present. When she was eighteen and in school in Sweden, having fallen madly in love with a handsome young Catholic professor from Norway, she was threatened with disinheritance from her strict family. It didn't deter her in the least, and she and her love, James Anderson, had eloped and come to America, settling in Mobile, Alabama. There was never a word between Rose and her family from that day on.

Mary's gentle, loving, Norwegian father was a carpenter here in America, a man who, if he accidentally hit his finger and let slip a "Damn," would immediately apologize. "Oh, forgive me, ladies, please."

Mary, the last and their youngest of seven girls and one boy was a baby the year the epidemic hit, 1921. The Great War – the terrible First World War – was over and the boys had come home. Dis-ease had brought disease. Sister Rose died from scarlet fever, Mary Magdalene from typhoid. Then the influenza epidemic hit. Their only son heard the doctor say he was well, only later to slip out of bed, catching a chill from the late afternoon air while sitting on a corner chatting with the rest of the boys. Two days later, he was dead. Mary still remembered the effects of its horror. Then father. All Mary's mother had left to give her was what she knew – the manners and education of her childhood aristocracy; and only with endless caring, she had tried to shield the remaining children from harsh reality.

The pains were stronger and closer together now. Her mouth felt hot and dry. Taking her balled-up fists, which were pressed under her legs, tight against the back of her knees, she brushed a piece of damp hair back off her face. With the other hand, she reached up over the left eyebrow and began to massage her forehead, pressing the skin together between the thumb and forefinger in a constant circular motion, as if trying to compress her very thoughts. She had better call Mrs. Combs and ask her to help her over to the hospital. But just one more minute, it was just across the road.

Preston whistled a new song, sailing along in his Ford, noting that a lot of new automobiles were whizzing along the highway. He also noted that a lot of his good, regular customers no longer even had any chickens. Although many yet suffered in poverty, not only in America, but the world over, those who could afford to play, indeed, did so. Whenever the warning sounds became too loud and clear, the players played all the harder to block out the warning note.

"Maybe my brother's right," Preston muttered. "Like R.W. says, you can't worry 'bout everybody. Get a damn ulcer. 'Course, he's a selfish son-of-a-bitch. If R.W. has a dollar left over, he's gonna spend it to play. 'Course there's a lot of nice things you can buy, now," Preston thought to himself. "Trousers with zippers on 'em 'stead of hooks. Colored shirts. Men's shorts with elastic tops."

He smiled at the thought that women seemed to be more feminine. Why, his sisters all said they could now wear what pleased them, from eye shades to ankle socks! He sure was happy ladies shorts were in to stay. Sun bathing habits had begun and cheap holiday cruises were in. Someday Mary and he might even take one.

He knew he should turn the car around and head in toward home to be with his family and lovely wife. God, he loved that woman. Yeah, he ought to go home, it being Thanksgiving and all. Especially with his child coming in any week now. But gosh darn, it was just another day and he'd sure as hell rather be busy keeping chickens and turkeys alive than rush home to eat a dead one! As the burning orange sun began to sing its last bar of the day, Preston continued driving, all the while, the rhyming, singing, Southern man was making up songs which he sang to himself:

"Riding here far away, Making money for

Another day, not going home, 'cause I want

to play, Yea, yea, yea..."

Most of the Taylor family made Mary feel foolish because she was definitely going to deliver her baby in the clean secure confines of a hospital. What was it they called the doctor? The gravedigger with forceps! Yes, that's right. They hadn't meant that she might end up in her grave, but what was the old saying? "The minute you were born, somewhere your grave was being dug for you." Well, she guessed there was no getting away from that, so you had better do in life whatever it was you're supposed to do. And right now, she knew what it was she had to do, all right.

She remembered what her Daddy used to say. "You don't have to worry about dyin'. A body didn't worry about being born, and that happened, and dyin'll happen too, you can bet your bottom boot on that. And if more people would spend their energy worrying about living and leading a good life, everything would be fine." Mary could hear his voice with the warm Norwegian accent and the deep infectious laughter that always followed.

Suddenly, her head went forward. It was as if all the preceding pains had joined forces. She couldn't get her breath and tried to cry out, but no sound. Then she sat straight up. The pain was gone, swiftly, and she was calm, completely, serenely calm, all in one instant. Her body was filled with a strength she had never tasted. She felt as strong as… but instantly she knew this calmness would be brief.

She opened the blue satin box on the dresser, and, taking up her rosary, wrapped it around her hand. She slipped a sweater over her shoulders.

As Mary shut the door behind her, she said to herself, "It is time for my child to join the rest of humanity." She paused for one brief second, "My heavens, we haven't decided on a name! . . . Suddenly, she knew that it wasn't going to be a boy, after all. It was going to be a girl….she just *knew!* The moment had come. "That's it," she said to herself, "I'll name her *Moment.*"

Fool's Gold

Years of potential lost life – that's what they call the difference between age 75 and the age a younger person dies. Accurately stated, that would be "dying prematurely." In a fast-paced and stressful city such as New York, a person's immune system can be put to the test on a daily basis. As you know, many diseases *begin in the mouth...*

In this city of one-and-a-half million, there are more than fifteen hundred dentists striving for success, something not all achieve. Thomas Vanderwyck, hailing from Tupelo, Mississippi, the little town famous as the birthplace of Elvis Presley – his birthplace as well – had garnered a scholarship to the Columbia University College of Dental Medicine. Following his graduation with honors, the good doctor set up his own small practice, becoming not only a board member of the American Dental Association but, in fact, one of the most successful and sought after oral surgeons in the city of New York. His office does it all: fillings, root canals, cosmetic dentistry, restorative work, porcelain veneers, implants, and oral surgery; the whole gamut. His reputation for philanthropic work in the poorer city hospitals is highly regarded.

But, unbeknownst to his patients, Dr. Vanderwyck does not always practice what he preaches. His well-to-do patients get what's referred to as the good stuff – what dentists call the real goods, while some of the doctor's struggling patients, as well as the charitable indigents, get the cheap amalgams. Dr. Vanderwyck declares all of it directly off his taxes as top-of-the-line goods.

"Who will ever know what's underneath those fillings, caps, and veneers?" he thought to himself with a smile as he gazed out the window across the park. "Oh God, one more week of looking into the gaping abyss of the human mouth and that blueprint of troubles they've chewed! Just one more week," he comforted himself with the thought as he chuckled.

"Uhhhmmmm," the young Korean boy moaned with a gurgle. Only then did Dr. Vanderwyck realize he'd actually laughed out loud and remembered he was in the middle of filling a cavity! Quickly covering his faux pas, he nodded to his assistant to wipe the spittle running down the young man's chin and insert the saliva ejector under his tongue to suction the excess water. He adjusted the rubber dam in the mouth, an aid to prevent the mercury amalgam from being swallowed. He always tried to be gentle – everyone is afraid of the dentist and all that drilling – probably because the mouth is so close to the brain. They feel they're giving up control and they are. Everyone hates giving up control. He removed the disposable tip, a sanitary requisite, off the drill.

"An amazing machine, this high speed drill," he marveled silently. "Jetting out lots of water to cool the heat generated by the 300,000 revolutions per minute drill, soothing while preventing nerve damage. Ohhh, how I wish I'd invented it. No matter, I've made my money," he reflected.

Turning to his assistant, who was holding the high-suction tip excavator next to the boy's tooth, he motioned as he spoke, "Hand it over."

"Excuse me, doctor?" Having done this many times before while in the midst of working on a patient, it continued to confuse her. He was taking full control of the patient.

He shot his head toward the room next door.

"I'm very concerned about Mrs. Goldstein." And before she could reply, he continued, "She's in pain, and very agitated. I need you to be with her. I can handle this. Please do as you're asked."

Reaching out and taking the excavator from her, he left no room for rebuttal as he turned away and continued his work. A little nervous, she awkwardly did as ordered. While apprehensive, the newly divorced pretty brunette with a six-year-old boy at home, valued her job.

The excavator was a tool to double-check, making sure that no debris had been left in the drilled-out cavity. However, in this case, as in many other cases, Dr. Vanderwyck wanted some of the debris left: the silver amalgam, a combination of mercury and silver that's been used for eons but banned in recent years. The huge scare about mercury poisoning and its long-term effects was being researched by a number of agencies.

"Absurd," he thought to himself.

He wiped the perspiration from the boy's forehead, and from his own. "Why am I perspiring?" he wondered.

After all, he'd done it this way so many times. Promising the patient to remove all the amalgam and replace it with a gold filling. Instead, he was leaving more than half and covering it with a gold top. He'd removed most of it and at any rate. The filling was so close to a nerve the boy might end up needing a root canal if he removed it all. That, of course, would be his justification should he ever be questioned.

The blunt truth was he used less gold than he charged for. It was a lucrative move that made him more money than even adding in a root canal. He'd made a bundle over the years – a by-God, incredible bundle! There were those who believed that gold covered over silver caused a galvanic current that would irritate the nerve, but Dr. Vanderwyck had never been subjected to a complaint.

He, of course, didn't play these games on the rich ones like Mrs. Goldstein in the other room. "Your whole mouth, my dear, has to be re-capped," he reported, "And I've rounded the price for you to a mere

$80,000."

He could buy a new car off this one patient – not the one he'd drive, but a very nice car. It was thanks to him that she'd look great and his conscience didn't pain him in the least, knowing that she could very well afford it. Many of his patients, as rich as she, also treasured his expertise.

Neither of his associates had ever guessed his gold or porcelain amalgam covering methods. The new owner of the clinic was bringing in both of his associates, Drs. Doshi and Grainger, as junior partners. Vanderwyck was glad. Knew it was something he should have done long ago, but he liked the big bucks too much to be rash enough to share the profits of his scam with partners.

Dr. Thomas Vanderwyck wasn't handsome, wasn't ugly. He was plain - very plain. It wasn't something that pleased him. It virtually gripped his loins. Slight of build, he'd been the youngest in a family of two girls and four strapping boys, mocked and pushed around both at school and at home. It was in the fields of Mississippi where he witnessed the life force ebb out of his father, who worked like a dog to put food on the table for his family. Thomas vowed success and he had, by-God, achieved it. And now, he was going to be the youngest dentist ever in New York City to retire – at age fifty!

Less than a week later, there he was, at last retired. He was high on life, feeling as if he were floating instead of actually standing beside his new 2012 silver metallic Porsche 911 GT2; a $231,700 monument to self-indulgence. "What the heck," he smiled to himself. "I've earned it."

Opening the door, he bowed proudly as an old-fashioned gentleman would, ushering his beautiful wife, Lahoma, into the passenger seat.

Turning back for the last time to the brownstone where they'd lived for the past fifteen years, he grinned ear-to-ear. He gave a final salute – not only to the stones in the building that had housed him and his family but also to life as he had known it.

"Not a bad life," he shrugged, "but damn good riddance." He laughed out loud as he got in and started the Porsche – 560 horsepower, 0 to 60 in 3.4 seconds – like a little boy, revving his new toy, taking off like a rocket through the Manhattan streets, exhilarated. He glanced at his wife, hoping for admiration.

Lahoma smiled her approval because that's what she knew he wanted. She silently prayed they'd get out of the city without killing anybody.

"What a crazy game," she thought. "We put speed signs up, daring drivers to exceed them, use our taxes to pay policemen to catch them, and pay judges to fine them. Then we allow ridiculously expensive machines like this one that can go 240 miles per hour. Good God, what a crazy world."

Tall, elegant, and always seemingly poised – so much so, that if she was pissed, no one ever knew. She was Iroquois – the Seneca tribe – and had been steeped with the need to control her emotions. She had learned well, raised a poor Indian child in a white man's world, often without shoes for her feet. On one desperate occasion, she saw her family cook and eat grass because they hadn't any other choices.

She loved her husband, though she was not in love with him. They'd married young and she'd been a faithful, perfect wife, perfect mother, giving him two children. Thomas Jr. was now 27, on his way to being a successful medical doctor, a Diplomat on the Board of Family Practice, and their 20-year-old daughter Cynthia was in her junior year at Columbia majoring in nutrition, one of Lahoma's favorite subjects. Thomas Sr. adores his wife.

Opening her Gucci purse and retrieving a nail file, she began to tend to her nails. Not because they needed it, but simply to have something to do with her hands. She wanted to hum, but they didn't like the same music, so she found a good jazz station and he was happy.

Heading west through New Jersey, they quickly crossed into

Pennsylvania, turned north, and finally saw the New York state line again as Interstate 81 wound its way through the picturesque countryside to Binghamton. Onward to U.S. Highway 20, they soaked in the magnificent rolling hills as they made their way to the beautiful Finger Lakes. Of course the hills were rolling, creating the lakes formed by glaciers dragging their way north to what is now the Great Lakes, northward to Lake Ontario.

Lahoma's face beamed with joy as the sign for the little community of Auburn, announcing a population of 28,574, whizzed by. The Vanderwyck's new home was just a short distance down the road on the way to Seneca Falls and the land of her ancestors. She knew it well and loved it, in spite of the poverty she had known in the early part of her life.

The anticipation whet her appetite. She's hungry and would much rather be riding in an old pick-up where she could kick back and have a sandwich and some coffee, but a Porsche isn't amenable to eats. She wouldn't have long to wait. The trip was only 4-and-a-half hours door to door – and Thomas was kicking that dog! The moving van wouldn't be there for another three hours.

As the beautiful, grey, three-story Victorian country house came into view, it almost took Thomas's breath away, just like the first time he'd seen it. It reminded him of a majestic Mississippi plantation home, similar to some haunting dream from the past. The lapped wood siding exuded inviting warmth and palest of lavender shutters graced each window with a friendly ambiance. A fantastic wrap-around porch replete with finial and spindles beckoned for toddies at sundown. There was even a swing on the porch. Situated in a virtual glen of white birch, pine, elm, and majestic oaks with a smattering of wannabe-charming trees, the house held court over the countryside. There was of all things, an actual red barn trimmed in white. Dr. Thomas Vanderwyck felt like he was coming home. He planned to be a gentleman rancher – Herefords,

Thoroughbred horses, a couple of dogs, and a workshop in the barn.

The brownstone had been more luxury than Lahoma had ever believed she'd have in this lifetime, but *this,* not in a hundred years would she ever have dreamed it possible. And she did love it. But there was one spot she loved more – their land up on the hill. Her husband had promised she could have it for her very own vegetable garden, like the one her grandmother had before she'd passed away. It had been so wonderfully satisfying and she was going to re-create it. The very thought sparked a child-like spirit within, dazzling her with a happiness she'd not yet tasted.

Firmly a month later, they were firmly ensconced in their home and spring was in the air. Lahoma gravitated to her garden plot – a half-acre of rich, loamy soil, already dry enough to plow. Forecasts verified that all dangers of frost had passed. She immediately set to work seeding hardy foods, planting radishes, green onions, peas, spinach, kale, chard, and all the lettuces. At the same time she had the workers help her plant the root vegetables that wouldn't come up until July: potatoes – Irish, sweet, and yam – rutabagas, turnips, carrots, and beets. In June she seeded the warm-weather vegetables: tomatoes, peppers, cucumbers, corn, string beans, squash, melons, and a pumpkin or two.

July found the garden with enough food to feed an army. Lahoma gave the surplus to the grateful Seneca Aid Society. The Vanderwyck's daughter, Cynthia was back from a sabbatical in Europe, home for a week, helping her mother with canning pickles, tomatoes, beans, and, being a professional nutritionist, she provided numerous wonderful recipes for the future.

Son Thomas Jr., the doctor, was studying in Italy and had yet to share their new existence.

Dr. Vanderwyck had never been happier, feeling healthier than ever with all the organic foods. *Living off the land.*

It was late September when Lahoma found herself having increasing trouble remembering: where she'd put her keys, glasses, purse, even her papers. Day by day the fog seemed to accelerate. She'd be in the middle of a sentence and suddenly just stop, unable to continue. Walk into a room and wonder why she was there. Her body felt sapped and even her muscles seemed to become weaker each day, finally taking to her bed and refusing to get up. Doctors didn't comprehend the mystery. Numerous tests couldn't diagnose any problem.

December found both the kids home, sadly not to celebrate Christmas – those plans were cancelled. It was clear Lahoma's demise was shockingly imminent. The family was with her in her last moments.

Dr. Vanderwyck was enraged when he found his son had ordered an autopsy.

"Can't you let your mother, my precious Lahoma, rest in peace?" They argued, but the deed was done before the order could be rescinded.

Thomas Jr. and Cynthia stayed on after the funeral. They were concerned about their father. He, too, seemed to be deteriorating rapidly.

At breakfast just after the New Year, Dr. Thomas Sr. angrily slammed the paper on the table, tucked his chin to his chest, and between gritted teeth, vehemently stuttered, "They're crazy. Out of their minds, all this talk about environmental pollutants and metals. Mercury poisoning indeed!"

"What?" Thomas Jr. looked up with interest as he sipped his coffee.

"All these damn articles insinuate we dentists aren't doing a good job removing silver amalgam. Stupid! It's *our fault* that deaths and severe health problems are being blamed on mercury? Ridiculous!" He banged the table with his fist, sloshing his coffee over its brim.

His son stared at him. "Dad, for God's sake, calm down. As a matter of fact, I want to do some tests on you. There is something to all those claims and..."

"Do you dare say that maybe your own mother had mercury in her mouth? My own *son* saying my inefficiency was responsible?" his voice rising an octave. "You think I'd allow mercury in my own wife's mouth? Are you insane?" He jumped up from the table.

"Holy Hannah! Dad, sit down," Junior ordered. "Nobody's blaming you for anything. I know you're the last person in the world who would allow mercury to be in Mom's mouth – or anybody's mouth, for that matter. I mean, good God, you're one of the greatest dentists on the planet. They should all be like you! Unfortunately, they're not!"

Sitting quietly back down, his father stared at the carpet on the floor, tracing designs with his shoe.

Junior spoke again.

"My college roommate, Jed, you met him, remember? He's a great guy – went to a dentist that did a half-assed job. I'd begged 'im, 'wait, go see my dad!' Uh uh, he didn't – that lazy bastard of a dentist that he went to only took out part of the amalgam and covered it with gold. Christ, in addition to the tongue, the muscle in the jaw is the strongest muscle in the body, but, you know that better'n anybody," he laughed. "It seems that every time Jed bit down, mercury vapors were being released – got sick as a dog! But he finally got it fixed. His uncle's a doctor."

Senior's thoughts suddenly became heavy, studying the different objects on the table, his fingers nervously dancing each to the other. Junior wondered if his dad, who had impeccable ethics, was embarrassed at the idea of a fellow colleague making that kind of mistake, or worse, doing it deliberately. He quickly tried to lift the conversation.

"But, hey, Dad," he muttered, "We're not even talking about dentistry. We're talking about plain, out-and-out pollution."

"Yes," his father whispered as he reached for the newspaper. "Yes, it's right here: New York Associated Press, Malcolm Ritter – *'Could it be the natural decline that afflicts older people is related to how much lead they absorbed decades before?'* And Dr. Philip Landrigan of the Mount Sinai School of Medicine in New York says, *'It makes sense that if a substance destroys brain cells in early life, the brain may cope by drawing on its reserve capacity until it loses still more cells with aging. Only then would symptoms like forgetfulness or tremors appear.'"*

Thomas Sr. laid the paper on the table and wiped his dry mouth with the back of his hand as he helplessly looked at his son and continued. "This… ah, Dr. Brian Schwartz at Johns Hopkins University appears to be some kind of expert and thinks normal aging could be exacerbated by exposure to ubiquitous environmental poisons like lead or other pollutants. Even the origin of Parkinson's disease is now being questioned. We may have done ourselves in, you think?"

Thomas Jr., shifting in his chair, sighed. "You know that Onondoga Lake, about two hours from here, they say it's full of mercury, salt, phosphorus, and ammonia, and it's been declared a hazardous waste site. Can you believe it?" Junior sucked in his bottom lip, contemplating whether or not he should continue with this subject matter. He'd been doing some research since his mother's demise.

Thomas Sr. waited expectantly as his son pulled a small notepad out of his pocket, flipped it open, and began to read.

"The now defunct Allied Corporation, presently owned by Honeywell International, is being held responsible for mass quantities of pollutants discharged directly into the lake. In 1970, a fishing ban was imposed and the Attorney General sued to stop the daily dumping of 25 pounds of mercury. Dad, that's 6,500 pounds a year – three-and-a-quarter tons!"

Shaking his head with disbelief, Junior continued, "In 1986, the Syracuse Works facility was dismantled and in 1989, New York State filed a lawsuit for contamination. In 1990, an undisclosed source was discovered discharging mercury into Nine Mile Creek – that's a tributary of the Lake! Then, in 1994 the lake bottom and surrounding sites were added to the Federal Superfund National Priority List as a hazardous waste site to be cleaned up." He pocketed the pad and studied his dad.

"Jesus." His father shook his head. "We moved here to avoid

pollution."

Junior cleared his throat. "Well, that lake's pretty far away but then, there are other places. For example, in the Adirondacks and in New England there are lakes, reservoirs, and cities contaminated. And look at the Catskills' reservoirs, supposedly safe to drink, yet, do you know they have signs warning pregnant woman and children not to drink the water and or eat any bass, trout, or other fish caught in the lake due to toxic materials?"

"Well, what the hell?" Thomas Sr. shook his head in disbelief. "It's okay for men?"

Junior laughed out loud, breaking the tension for both of them. Then he shrugged. "Song birds are dying. If the birds start dying, the insects will multiply and all kinds of new diseases will begin. We'll slide down a slippery slope to health risks for everyone in the area."

"Why?" His father with a tinge of sadness, tilted his head, stared at Junior. and questioned, "Why are you fixated on pollutants?"

"Because," he answered simply and sadly, "Because of all the symptoms listed in Mother's chart. I can't find the source and I'm concerned about you, Dad. I want to do some tests."

"Damn it! They didn't find *anything in her blood!"*

"You don't find heavy metals in the blood!" Junior's voice elevated with anger. "These damn doctors can't see past their nose. But I can do a "challenge test" on the urine and..."

"I don't want quackery!" Yelling, his father interrupted.

"This is not quackery, its inclusivity!" his son yelled back as he stood. "I am an AMA doctor who also happens to believe, for damn good proven reasons, in alternative modalities – you don't throw out the baby with the bath water! In order to find a cure you have to find the cause. Jesus, Dad, our traditional medicine is China's alternative and her traditional medicine is only barely our alternative, mostly scoffed at, and you know what? Chinese medicine has been around a hell of a

lot longer than ours; thousands and thousands of years longer. I wish to God I had gotten here before it was too late for Mom. Well, anyway, it's not too late for you, so I'm going to run a few tests. Dammit, don't you know I love you?"

Thomas Sr. tried to look away. He didn't want his son to see tears in his eyes.

"One other thing, Dad."

"What?"

"What's this about these crazy nightmares the nurse tells me you've been having?"

"Oh, that? It's nothing. Just like everybody else – some bad dreams," said Thomas Sr.

"No, no. Don't do that. Tell me. I want to know. What's in the dreams?" He sat back down and leaned forward, supporting his face with his hands as he peered into his father's being.

"I... ah... have this weird dream. Doesn't seem to have anything to do with your mother or her death, but I'm in these odd clothes, old-timey American, but nice – kind of like the late 1800s or early 1900s; well-dressed. And I'm standing outside this structure that seems to be some kind of mine. It's always the same exact mine – so real, I could draw it.

"Anyway," Thomas Sr. continued, "I'm a very important person and people look up to me. Some people who are coming out of the mine seem dazed, foggy. And you can see this strange pain in their eyes as they look at me. I feel so... I don't know, guilty, and I want to say something, to explain, but I can't get the words out. The people are *waiting for the words*. It's horrible. I'm choking. I try to cry out, then, I wake up screaming! Same dream, time after time. It started about two weeks before your mother died." Vanderwyck's shoulders began to shake, withheld tears from spilling forth.

His son quickly put his arms around him, attempting to

comfort him.

"It's okay, Dad. It's okay, but... hey, I have an idea." Cocking his head, Thomas Jr. rubbed his chin thoughtfully. "Do me a favor, will you? When you feel like it, just sit down and draw the dream, draw the place – that mine, as best you can. And anything else you recall."

During the following week, Dr. Thomas Vanderwyck, Jr., though he couldn't comprehend the connection, spent his days researching an intuitive theory. He even hired a detective who turned out to be quite valuable.

Junior helped his father into the passenger seat of Senior's Porsche, thinking, "Dad'll enjoy the trip more if he's in his own car." Junior got behind the wheel.

"Getting corrupted is easy," Junior thought to himself with a grin. He understood why men love Porsches as he felt the power behind the wheel, taking the curves along the highway like a smooth sailing vessel.

An hour and a half later, at their destination, his father staring ahead, bolted up straight. As he stepped out onto the ground, his face was suddenly rapt with attention and a wild recognition.

"This… this is…" he stammered as he walked slowly toward the hill. "The *place*!" His heart raced as he said, "This place is… my dream! My God, where are we?"

Thomas Jr. spoke slowly, studying his father carefully all the while, "I, ah, took your drawing to the library, several times, and then one day I accidentally met up with one of the elderly librarians who knew it. Dad, she clearly recognized your drawing. Maybe you'd seen it in a book or something?"

"Nope," his dad muttered quietly. "No, never seen it anywhere except in my dream."

"Because," Junior continued, "There's only one old mine anywhere around here in any direction. This is it. And it's old – like a hundred years old. Most people don't even know it's a mine, but no one around these parts will build anywhere close, as you can see." Waving his arm at the panorama, he continued, "There are no houses anywhere on all this beautiful land! Strange, huh? People are still scared of possible vapors if they're too close!"

Thomas Sr. seemed to go dizzy and swooned. His son grabbed him, suggesting they leave immediately, worried that the trip was too much after all.

"No," his father insisted in a tone almost too firm. "Tell me. WHAT is this place?"

"Ah, uh…" Junior coughed trying to regain his voice. "It's a mine, named *Dreamy Daze*. It got its name because when the workers came out of the mine after a long day, they were in a daze. All of them and most of their families died here."

Thomas took in a deep breath. "I've NEVER been here before in my life!" his father spit out emphatically with a desperation Junior could feel. Senior's brow was wet with perspiration and his body trembled as he turned to his son, his eyes pleading. "You believe me, don't you? Do you believe that I've *never* been here before?"

"Yes, Dad," Junior replied sincerely but with deep concern. "I do believe you."

"And I don't ever want to come here again!" And slowly turning away, he demanded, "This doesn't feel good. I want to go now. Please."

Thomas Jr. helped his shaken father back to the car. Their ride home was ominously silent. Junior tried once or twice to converse, but Senior didn't respond. He just stared out the window and then, finally, putting his head back against the seat, closed his eyes, shutting out the world.

During the next few days, Thomas Sr. was withdrawn, on some inner voyage, emanating an untouchable stupor that came from within, not just the growing illness. He had no way of sorting out what he was feeling. Even if that were possible, Dr. Thomas Vanderwyck, Sr. may not have wanted to comprehend the growing realization in the furthest reaches of his soul.

His son was at loss. Conducting his own tests he found it – mercury poisoning.

The insidious metal had, as always, attacked the spinal chord, working its way to the brain and the central nervous system. Junior pursued every avenue he could think of to de-tox his father's body, including chelation with EDTA – a process used by many wise holistic doctors to remove heavy metals from the blood system. But that particular treatment relied on strong kidneys needed to filter the toxins and carry them, in the urine, out of the body. Unfortunately, his father's kidneys were failing, therefore treatments were limited.

Time was running out, and even if he couldn't save his father, he wanted to know – had to know – the truth, whatever the truth was. He believed in the furthest regions of his soul that his father's dreams and the mine itself were somehow intricately interwoven in the unfolding drama of his life, but try as he might, he couldn't make one possible connection. After persistent but fruitless research, he was left, in his mind, with only one possible choice.

The two men, invited by Junior, who knocked at the Vanderwyck's door three days later, were top specialists in their field. As medical doctors, their respected and admired reputations preceded them. Dr. Carmona was the Italian doctor with whom Thomas Jr. had been privileged to study for the last year, and Dr. Weinberg was an M.D. from Washington, D.C., whom Dr. Carmona had persuaded to accompany him today. Among their sterling credentials, they were considered to be two of the top ten "Past Life Regressors" in the world.

Thomas Jr. was simply going to tell his father that the men were using hypnosis to diagnose and heal. But Dad was a wise old fox, got the picture immediately, and would have none of it. Thomas Vanderwyck, Sr. had been raised a hard-shell Baptist. Religion was the one and only constant in his life as a child. That little house of Sunday worship had been his only joy, he was never going to give it up – even if he had cheated people on their gold fillings – even if he hadn't been to church in years. The thought of this past life nonsense was akin to some sort of devil-worship as far as he was concerned.

Whatever it was, something in another one of his dreams or simply weighing alternatives, who in God's name knew, but Senior, to their amazement, suddenly did a 180 degree turnaround. Very early the next morning, a chill permeating the library, Junior and Drs. Carmona and Weinberg were having a discussion. To their surprise, Dr. Vanderwyck, Sr., shaking, leaning on his cane and tottering slowly forward – greeted them in a quiet manner as he whispered, "I want you doctors to help me. Please!"

Dr. Carmona calmly, patiently and competently began the process. Soon Thomas Vanderwyck, Sr. was in a deep trance. As Dr. Weinberg and Junior took notes, Dr. Carmona led Thomas Sr. back, into a previous existence, letting him choose the date, place, and incidents as he saw fit. Interestingly, Thomas Sr. immediately drifted to the lifetime wherein he chose as the point of most importance... *the mine.*

Now a skeptic might say, "Oh, yes, of course, but he'd had these dreams and then seen the mine!" While that might be the usual logic, the taped session revealed much more. While under hypnosis, Thomas Sr. prattled on with names, dates, faces, and places which were later checked and validated for authenticity. There was no way he could have previous conscious knowledge of the tale he spun that day of one hundred years ago.

On tape, Thomas Sr. gave his name as J.W. Arsenault, a French Canadian, and he described a strawberry birthmark on top of his head, duly recorded on his birth paper. He said his mother had craved strawberries and hadn't gotten any because it was winter. He gave his wife's name, Claudette, describing her along with a specific number of personal incidents, the names of his six children, their schools, the names of their favorite teachers and their avocations. He commented on his wife's surgery along with the name of the surgeon. He gave the address of their home, the names of their three horses, two dogs and their cat. He provided the names of his two investors: an Irishman, Mr. Shea, who became his manager and supervised the men, working with them, and a Scotsman, Mr. MacLeish, who was the accountant. However, he himself was the discoverer, owner and developer of the "Dreamy Daze" mercury mine.

Cinnabar, the bright red mercury rich ore, is mucked out of mines and processed in giant retorts. During the process, mercury vapors permeate the air, unseen and unnoticed. Little did they know at the time, prolonged exposure is usually fatal. Mr. Shea, his investor and manager, died a horrible death – total deterioration of every muscle and the brain – as did hundreds of miners, their families, and others in the area. The constant exposure to mercury took its deadly toll and too few knew its long term consequence.

And so it went, day after day, year after year. Arsenault knew that he should close the mine. His denial continued too long and his greed had been too strong.

"One more year, just one more year," he had continued to sing to himself even though the deaths of his workers had been proof enough.

After Dr. Carmona's session, Dr. Thomas Sr. wanted to know *exactly* what he'd said. He was extremely attentive as the doctors shared the tape with him. He listened quietly and gently thanked them. Without question or comment, he rose and left the room. Later, he avoided any discussion of the matter – refused it – and in those last few days of his life the subject was taboo.

Thomas Jr. and Cynthia, both heartbroken at the loss of their beloved parents, lay their father to rest beside their mother. The son, a great doctor in his own right, felt like a failure. They had to stay in order to settle the estate, and Thomas Jr. found sleep a very hard-to-get commodity. He couldn't understand. Utterly frustrated, continued asking himself that one question.

"What in the hell did this whole past life have to do, if anything, with Mom's and Dad's deaths? If there is a connection," Thomas Jr. pondered, "God knows, I'm missing it."

Shortly after, one night, tossing and turning until the early morning, he suddenly sat bolt upright.

The next day was spent in the small town library amidst very old newspaper clippings. Finally, Junior arrived at the target of his search, discovering exactly what he feared he would: *Those poor families couldn't afford coffins. The deceased bodies were wrapped in simple potato sacks, then interred directly into the ground. There was only one cemetery within a hundred miles.* And the connection was crystal clear.

That "Old Cemetery" was now Lahoma's garden, that beautiful half-acre on the hill. That dark, rich, loamy soil was interspersed with the mercury of long-decayed cadavers. What a fateful turn. Thomas Vanderwyck, Sr. had purchased his dream retirement estate where a hundred years ago, the *Dreamy Daze* mining company buried the families that worked the mine – all of whom died of mercury poisoning exacerbated by J.W. Arsenault's reluctance to face the facts of which only he and few others were aware.

Thomas, Jr. peered into the blue expanse, marveling at the billowing clouds that brushed their way past the 747's wing as they began their descent into Rome. He was, at last, returning to his last year of internship with the amazing Dr. Carmona. The eight-hour flight had given him plenty of time to mull the karma he thought he understood.

His dear mother Lahoma had been a firm believer in reincarnation, and while she had been careful never to contradict the Baptist theology that meant so much to Dad, she was, nevertheless, glad to discuss her ancestor's teachings anytime Junior had asked – interesting conversations. Apparently, the soul's path of living many lifetimes enabled it to gain the education needed to evolve spiritually, even though not all souls evolve at the same pace.

It kind of makes sense, he mused. As his mother had explained it, your body is like an automobile that carries you from one place to another so you can do what you have to do. When that car wears out, you get another vehicle – a Porsche, a Ford, a Toyota, a van, a truck, a motorcycle, or even a bicycle. Mom and the people before her believed that earth is God's school for humans, and unfortunately, you don't progress from kindergarten to a Master's degree in only one lifetime. Evolving depended on their choices.

"There's just one damn thing that doesn't make sense," he thought. Anger still percolated throughout his mind as he pondered his mother's wisdom. "If, and I mean *if*, there's anything to all this whole Arsenault – Vanderwyck circle of drama, if my father in a past life was in some crazy way responsible for people's deaths from mercury, didn't he damn well make up for it? If there's any way on God's green earth that this nonsense is really true, wouldn't he have made amends by choosing to come back in this life as a dentist? It would have given him the opportunity that he needed – helping people by his charitable work and taking mercury out of people's teeth! Jesus, he was the best!"

From forty-thousand feet one can see a long way, taking in quite a lot. But sometimes in life, it's hard. Hard to see the big picture, or the whole picture.

Life just wasn't fair. Or was it?

Great Day for a Train Ride

Rush Street in Chicago is appropriately named. People rush, alright – to get everything they want in the way of entertainment, from road shows and stage plays to nightclubs and, well, vices to fulfill every indulgence, shadowing their paths. The kid slunk stoop-shouldered through the streets, trying to be inconspicuous, convinced that everyone was staring at him. He couldn't be more wrong.

No one noticed the kid because no one really cared. Maybe, somewhere, he knew that, and it made him feel even worse. The kid was all of sixteen-and-a-half, and the preceding years hadn't been too kind on his developing manhood.

His family had just moved up to Chicago from the Mississippi Coast, from the little town of Biloxi, where the kid had been really happy and felt so secure because he knew everybody. Now, here he was, not knowing anybody. Trying to make friends and to impress his fellow students – it was a near impossible feat. And to make things worse, as of recent, he'd somehow contracted, of all things, ringworm, and of all places, on his head. The doctors made him shave off all his hair. Trying to hide his little shiny bald head, he'd taken to wearing this sock cap but it only served to entice the other kids to try and pull it off. They'd dubbed him a new name, "Bean-head."

Following that crisis, the kid was finally allowed to date. Well, that is, if you can call escorting fashionable young ladies born of wealthy families in the suburb of Glencoe, Illinois to high school parties dating.

The kid may not have fit in, but his family certainly did. They were a philanthropic family. His grandfather – his mother's father – was originally from Greenwood, Mississippi. Grandfather had conducted business for a lifetime in Chicago and lived in the elegantly grand, three-story house on the hill. He was a self-educated man, having come over from Scotland with his parents, farmers, settling in the Southland.

Barely turning seventeen, Grandfather had gone off on his own, up north, to the big city. He had begun his career working as a janitor for one of Chicago's famed department stores. Later in life, diligently persevering his way up that long ladder, he had become that same company's president and major stockholder. Grandfather was the patriarch of the family – the accountant and organizer – thereby allowing his brothers to concentrate on their artistic side. One brother became an internationally acclaimed artist and the other brother became Poet Laureate of the United States, his new adopted country.

Grandfather married an elegant lady who had helped found a young women's college which was to later become the top tier of women's schools in the country – Wellesley College. At the time of their marriage, even though he had sometime earlier risen above the position of janitor, they didn't have a lot of money. Their existence was certainly nothing like the lifestyle he would later be capable of providing. They raised two children. A daughter – the kid's mother – who was the apple of Grandfather's eye, and an adopted son who generated a bit of mystery. He was the illegitimate son of someone in the family. Few ever knew.

While the daughter had been engaged to a fine young man, she spied the Governor's son, held her breath for a moment and had a change of heart. She said, "I'm going to marry him, have three children, and someday live near Daddy in a big brick home," which is exactly what she ultimately did. She joined with this man, a top lawyer, the son of the first non-Mormon governor of the State of Utah, who later held a prominent position in the Roosevelt White House. Her husband had been hired to represent the entire holdings of the largest pecan nursery in the entire world, down in his adopted state of Mississippi, so he enticed her to move there. They had three children.

The kid was the middle child. When his older brother was born, there was a lot of fanfare. The Robert Millers have a son! Then the kid was born, not a lot of hullabaloo. Later, they had a girl. The Robert Millers have a daughter! It was hard for the kid to get his share of attention. He always seemed to be trying to measure up to his siblings.

It was hard to live up to his big brother, who seemed to do everything right – college football hero, following Grandfather's footsteps in the family business, a perfect dresser, perfect manners, everything perfect: the star heir-apparent. Live up to that while protecting his little sister, being responsible for her? It was a drag.

His mother had finally persuaded her husband to move the family back from Mississippi and right next to her Daddy in Glencoe, Illinois, right outside Chicago. Good-bye to the friendly buddies, happy hills and surfing waves he'd known as home, but at least now the kid was allowed to date. Take a girl out, take her home. Maybe a goodnight kiss – maybe – but no parking, no petting, no nothing. After all, his mother explained, he had a heritage to live up to – a reputation.

Yeah. He'd tried to comply – to be the gentleman they were priming him to be. Like the time he'd taken out a girl he really liked and they'd gotten all steamed up – but he'd waited, like a good boy, until they arrived back at her house, in fact, at her own door, before he zeroed in for that hot goodnight kiss he'd been pining for. Yeah, he'd gotten that kiss alright, and something more he hadn't expected. He got stuck!

He wore braces, as did she, and they somehow managed to interlock the metal in their mouths. There they stood with their braces entwined, stuck like two copulating dogs until the adults, amidst great laughter, got them unstuck.

"Well," the kid groused, "I'm sick of all of it."

While his dad was in the shower, he quickly slipped a fifty out of his father's wallet. "Dad'll never miss it," he thought to himself, "Heck, he's too busy to even count his money. Well, screw 'em – heritage and all. Tonight I'm going to become a man!"

He was going to get laid and Rush Street was the destination.

The girls "rushed" along the pavement, giggling about the old man who said he only had two dollars - he was horny and life was cruel. Didn't they have any sympathy in their heart for an old man? What were young girls made of these days, anyway? They teased him, made him think it was his lucky day, then they called him an old fart and ran away to play.

They could afford to take time for fun and games. Last night had been a good one. Emily had earned three hundred and sixty bucks. So, to hell with the rest of the week, she didn't have to sweat it. It was all bacon for the other six days, a nice change from the all-to-common leaner weeks.

Some times were profitable. Conventions paid well. Emily and Lois made two-thousand each a month ago, doing their special act. Emily, the younger, had in some ways, even though it didn't show, become an old woman at only twenty-two. Lois was twenty-nine and the grind showed. She was a redhead, skinny, shrewish on top of bitter. Very different from Emily, an adorable brunette, the epitome of the all-American girl-next-door. Epitome, yes, but Emily's modus operandi as she explained to Lois, was, "Live for today – might be the only day you have left to breathe. Get what you can while you can and to hell with everybody else."

"Hey, Emily," Lois laughed, "I'm either crazy or there's a beanie kid following us. He's hiding behind the corner."

"See!" she exclaimed. "He just poked his head out again."

Emily stopped, pretended she was fixing her stocking and waited.

The kid peeked around the corner again.

"Oh, God, did they see me?" the kid thought. "They can't be hookers – probably college girls down here to take in a play. Shit. I'm going to make a damn fool of myself. Get into trouble sure as shooting as I always do. I can't fail this time – I just can't."

All the kids in his class had been laid – or so they said – except him. He wondered if he would always be the odd man out.

"Hey, Emily," Lois whispered, "Did ya see 'im?"

"Yeahhhhh," Emily replied in a hushed voice. "Jesus, he's just a kid."

"Maybe he wants a trick," Lois laughed. "First the old man and now this. Shall we go in the charity business? You wanna educate him, honey?"

They both began to giggle.

"He's a skinny little thing," Emily muttered, having observed his last full body glance around the corner.

"Yeah," Lois laughed. "If he was on top of ya, he'd feel like a gnat. If you moved, he might fall off."

"Ah, hell," Emily whispered, "Let's go find out what he's up to."

The kid's palms perspired against his jeans pocket. His heart felt as if it would explode. "Did they see me? This is stupid. I'm going to make a damn fool of myself. Well, just one more peek. Maybe they've moved on. Maybe I've waited too long," he thought.

As the kid's ear brushed the corner of stone for one last look, his blue searching eyes stared into a pair of lovely inviting green eyes. The long black lashes reminded him of the fans of a goddess waving invitingly at him.

"Helloooo," Emily smiled.

She reminded him of his sister – this girl couldn't be a hooker – he'd made a terrible mistake. He wanted to run but his feet were glued to the pavement. His knees felt like magnets pulling each against the other through his blue jeans. His head was hot and he felt the blood flushing through his face. He wanted to die. Not live another second on this planet. Just evolve into a molecule of air, floating with no sound, no feeling, no blame, no guilt, and no game.

"Do I know you?" the girl smiled. Her voice felt rather than sounded like the touch of velvet. Oh, God, he'd made a terrible mistake.

"Are you looking for a trick, honey?" the other one asked.

The kid didn't like this other girl. A TRICK? WERE THEY THE REAL THING? Was it possible? His mouth fell open and he just stared.

Emily smiled, "Look, sugar, come back when you're older and can afford us. OK?"

They turned and started away. He couldn't take his eyes off the rhythm of the younger one's hips – like a lullaby of some ancient song he'd heard long ago.

"Listen," he called out sheepishly. "I've only got fifty, but I could get more."

The girls stopped in their tracks. "Fifty?" Lois glanced quizzically at Emily as they turned. Twenty-five was the going rate for a quickie. Where in hell had this beanie little kid gotten his mitts on a fifty?

His heart was throbbing in his throat as he watched them talk it over. Then they turned towards him and approached him with a look of serious business on their faces.

"Jesus," he thought to himself, "I'm gonna die!"

The relationship that ensued was more than a quickie. The kid became friends of sorts with the girls. At first, they couldn't really do anything with him. He tried, oh, how he tried, but it was all too overwhelming. Nevertheless, there were many stolen fifties lifted from his father's wallet and, of course, his father never noticed. When his mother asked, "Son, where are you going?"

"Down to Rush Street to see the hookers," he replied.

"Oh," his mother laughed, "you're getting so bad!" She was charmed by the devilishness of her little boy who was growing up, never dreaming that he was, after all, using honesty as his weapon.

The girls, to entice his sexuality, had showed him their specialty – a lesbian act they used for conventions. Of course they faked it and the old fools thought they were really doing it. Showed what they knew!

But for the kid, he was special, no faking, the real thing, just for him. Wasn't that exciting, just for him? Imagine, he turned on two ladies all at once. Complete control. Oh, what a man he was! The fact that he hadn't gone all the way with either one – well, what the hell, that was beside the point. After all, they said he was in control and what a man they said he was. They oughta know, after all, they tricked with a lot of men and were paid for it, too.

While they pleasured and played with each other, he watched and did what young boys often do. He was drawn to their beauty. Could there be a sin in that? And he was helping them, wasn't he? Yes sirree, he diddled while they played, and he paid. They could pay their rent off him. Wasn't that a lot better than fucking a lot of pretentious old bastards they couldn't stand to have touch them? In a way, he was saving them. Saving hookers, how about that? His way of keeping up the old heritage. Saving the basis of humanity and doing his thing. Everybody was happy. Jesus, he was helping to save hookers! He sure as hell couldn't get anybody pregnant this way and he was having a lot of fun. His complexion was even clearing up, Dad wasn't missing the ole bucks, the girls in Glencoe thought he was the perfect escort, and he was cumming good and saving hookers. Shit, man, it was a great life if you could live it and he was living it!

Besides, he didn't have those confusing, inappropriate, middle-of-the-night dreams about his mother anymore. God, the guilt he'd felt from those dreams. Perhaps that would eventually go away, too. In time.

The kid liked Emily a lot. He had this fantasy of marrying her and changing her life. Why not – anything was possible. One day when Lois wasn't there, the kid mustered all his courage and shared his plan. Big mistake.

"Look, kid," Emily said angrily, "don't put me down for being a hooker, see. I don't need saving. So don't go getting sooo Mr. Goody Upright Glencoe Snob on me! In fact, I do the saving – as much as any damn doctor. I mean, I don't just do good for myself. The guy last night had a hell of a lot of problems and if it wasn't for me he'd probably gone home and beat the hell out of his wife. Instead he pissed on me."

Emily threw her head back and roared with laughter. Then she sat up and earnestly tried to explain, "I put on my raincoat and a fish bowl over my head and let 'em go," she laughed. "But, I didn't laugh at him. That's the thing in my profession, understanding."

The kid blushed, uncomfortable with her honesty.

"Listen, kid," Emily stood up, stretching her body like a cat. "If that guy gets his jollies by pissing on a raincoat and wants to pay me a thousand dollars…"

"A THOUSAND DOLLARS!" the kid interrupted.

"That's right, sugar," Emily continued. "Who's he hurting? You wouldn't understand. Your folks got money." A sad smile crossed her face, remembering. "My parents were both alcoholics. This one weekend, when I was three, they forgot about me. There wasn't any food in the refrigerator, so I ate out of the trash can. Oh well, that wasn't the only time I went hungry.

"Once I went next door to ask the nice man who lived there if I could please have something to eat. I was starving. He took me inside. He had some cookies, alright. He crumbled them up and put them on his cock. He said that if I licked the crumbs off, then I could have a whole handful of cookies. Yeach."

Emily sighed and went into the kitchen to put on some coffee. Later, when Lois came back and they got fifty off the kid, they were going to give him a treat and let him take them to a movie.

The following week, Lois was arrested for prostitution. An irate customer – a friend of someone in the D.A.'s office – had felt that Lois hadn't earned her money and he was going to show that little bitch where to get off.

But Emily, she was smart. She wasn't going to fight those staunch politicians she entertained. Nor was she going to start asking for favors. Favors had to be repaid. She simply packed and left.

When no one answered the door, the kid pounded on it. There was no response to his fist, but the door was unlocked. He wandered through the vacant rooms and stared at the empty closet. His heart pounded in his ears as he listened to the landlady repeating, "Yes, Lois is in jail and Emily's gone. No forwarding address."

"No forwarding address? Nothing!" he thought, as he turned away quickly to hide the gathering tears. Outside, he began to run, away from his love – all lost. His friend was gone and she hadn't even left him a note, a goodbye. He ran so he wouldn't think, wouldn't feel. He ran.

Emily stared out the window of the train as the world passed by.

"What the hell," she thought, "New York will be better pickings anyway. Lois'll be alright, she can take care of herself."

She reflected on her life - the time she'd spent in Chicago, the different customers, and for a brief second the kid flashed before her.

"Funny kid," she thought, "So sensitive a young man."

Oh well, the time they'd given him, he was better off than staying curled up in a corner in his rich Glencoe home, all alone with a copy of Playboy magazine. Ah, what the hell, it was no skin off her nose, and her thoughts danced on to other memories.

How was she to know that she had instigated within the boy's budding manhood a karmic circle in his life that would entwine his emotions – his deeply imbedded memory of a forever lost first love. The young woman couldn't comprehend how her impact on the kid further limited his already damaged ability for achieving the potential of love within his future marriage – thereby ending in a disastrous divorce –

causing his own child to grow up subjected to only rare visits from his father. The karmic chain continues unbroken.

Emily never stopped to wonder who helped start those circles in her own life. She gathered herself up and wandered toward the dining car to see what action she could brew up. Maybe she'd get it when she grew up.

If.

Lucky Enough to be in Life

The afternoon sunbeams filtered through dried tracks of yesterday's rain on the window, bursting through countless prisms that warmed the unpretentiously charming house in the Louisiana Delta. Sanguine sparkles danced across the flame-coppered locks of an impish, freckle-faced boy, playing alone in the modest living room. The six-year-old, prone on the floor, holding an old broom handle, was pointing it at the sleeping dog. Bam, bam, bam! I got yah, yah damn towel head."

Shocked, his mother Essie stopped cold over the breakfast of hominy grits and bacon she was serving up. Ezra, the boy's father, looked up from his morning paper. Distress crept across his face as he gently called, "Son, c'mon over here, please."

"Ahwoooeee, gonna catch it now," said his eleven-year-old sister Irma Jean, giggling with her mouth full. She continued in a singsong voice, "You said a curse word – gonna go to hell!"

"Hush up right now, Missy," her momma clipped.

Ezra, glancing at his daughter, spoke gently. "All kinds of hell in this world, honey. Be careful," he winked. "Judging is one kind of hell in and of itself!"

Jonathan scooted up off the floor and hurrying across the short distance, started talking as he entered the kitchen. "But, but, I heard Uncle N.W. say it," he protested even before the first word of reprimand was spoken.

His father, looking 'im straight in the eye, replied, "Your uncle N.W.'s an idiot. Is that what you want to be? Like him?"

The boy, squirming, replied, "No sir. But Daddy, Uncle N.W's not alone – lotsa the kids call them Iraqis *towel heads* and I…"

"Jonathan," his daddy's firm tone brought him to silence. "The man who shot me wasn't wearing a towel on his head. No, son, he was wearing a helmet, just like I was." His father sighed and then, letting the boy off the hook, smiled as he changed the subject. "I won't probably get back home in time to catch your soccer practice but I'll be at the game Saturday – done told Mr. Johnson I'm not working."

Jonathan grinned ear to ear, showing his two missing teeth. "Hey Dad, let me go with you today, please?" Hopeful, he climbed up on his father's lap.

"If he goes, I wanna go, too," Irma Jean chimed in. "Boys get to do everything – not fair."

"You kids are going to school," Essie announced, pouring her husband another cup of coffee. "Your daddy's paying for schooling and that's where you're going."

Irma Jean cocked her head curiously. "What paying? Mama, it's a public school."

Her mother drew in her breath aghast. "Don't you sass your mother, young lady!"

"No, M'aam," the girl responded. "I didn't…"

"What your mother means is," her daddy interrupted as he got up, "the money we spend on books, lunches, school clothes, and all the rest of things. That's one of the reasons I work." He smiled as he stood tall and erect. "So you can go to school and learn!"

Ezra crossed over to the corner coat rack, retrieving his light brown suede jacket and favorite brimmed hat, his family oblivious to his limp; they'd grown accustomed to it over time. Sometimes the pain barked at his left leg, his prosthetic attached at the knee, but he'd learned in the past year to live with this discomfort in his life.

"You didn't eat all yoah breakfast, Ezra," Essie scolded lovingly, shaking her glistening mane of red hair. "You've got a long hard day, honey, you gonna need sustenance."

"Later, sweetie," he laughed. Nodding to the children, he said, "C'mon, grab your lunch pails," as he hugged his precious wife good-bye. "I'll wait with you for the school bus."

Their peaceful home in St. Tammany parish was twenty-seven miles straight across from New Orleans along Lake Ponchetrain's Causeway. As he drove, Ezra inhaled the crisp morning air and studied the land. He'd been raised next door in Mississippi, but for a few years now, this was his home. The rocky shoreline, the magnificent pines popping out of nowhere, all held their purchase along the red clay hills he loved. The green valleys patch-worked into hundreds of acres of freshly plowed fields and sprouting crops garnished the countryside.

Ezra Overmeyer was of German heritage. His ancestors settled in the Southland in the late 1700's. His family's legacy, as far back as he could remember, was soldiering. Great Granddaddy Wilhelm fought in the Civil War, his Granddaddy Gottlieb had been killed in World War I, and his daddy Ezekiel was a veteran of World War II. Uncles and cousins – alive and dead – had fought in everything from the Korean War and Vietnam to the Gulf War. Now here he was, the Overmeyer's eldest son, freshly back from the Iraq War.

Ezra hated wars. He didn't believe in them unless you had to defend your own country. He'd done his duty, in spite of his beliefs, and brought back a real souvenir – his fake leg. He considered himself one of the lucky ones. Of his parents' three sons, unfortunately, he was the only one available to carry on the family's tradition of service.

Joe Bob, the middle son, just reached age twelve when he lost his life celebrating with some classmates at the school picnic. Nobody knew the community lake had a suck hole. His drowning death was grieved over forever and a day.

Maybe that's why Teddy, the youngest, was always getting into some kind of mess. He was just trying to get his share of attention and going about it the wrong way. Teddy and another boy had been caught in a teenage prank – siphoning gas from a big truck parked overnight at the town's only gas station. A stupid childish prank, but he got caught, big time. It was a truck belonging to the federal government, and Teddy, at age 15, was sent to a Juvenile Detention Center where he would spend his whole teenage life.

The tragic part was his daddy could've gotten him off the federal rap, but he'd said, "No. Punish him. My boy committed the crime, let 'im do the time."

His daddy probably thought he was doing the right thing, but it'd always seemed to Ezra, that maybe his daddy, somehow, had been looking for somebody – anybody – to pay for Joe Bob's death.

Jail hadn't taught Teddy a damn thing. He was a mess when he came out – robbed a post office of all things and was now back in the pen.

Ezra proudly graduated summa cum laude from Mississippi State University with a B.A. in Business Management. He immediately married Essie, his beautiful childhood sweetheart.

He decided to change their lives. They moved up to New York City, and Ezra became a successful stockbroker with a prestigious Wall Street firm. He loved it. Then, three years later and less than two years after the September 11, 2001 terrorist attack on the Twin Towers, America found herself pulled into another war and a shocked Ezra found himself and his Army Reserve buddies – family tradition, you know – on their way to Iraq, of all places.

They were part of the 49th Infantry Division, one of the first to be sent over. One of his best friends, a terrific guy in the 155th Battalion, Company B, was one of the first to die. They had two weeks training and straight to Bagdad, the Green Zone, searching buildings and homes. Then, a few months later, they moved out to the desert towns where the fighting was sporadic but ruthless, dealing primarily with the Taliban and terrorists. It was horrible.

One of the things Ezra couldn't understand was why nobody in Iraq was protecting those kids on the street, those left without any family. Left to wander about looking for food while seen as prey for perverts and slave traffickers, many were grabbed and spirited away to who knows what – little lost souls.

He also couldn't understand why the government spent money the way it did. Like putting up the money to build a small jailhouse in Iraq that ended up costing ten times more than any jailhouse that size had ever cost anywhere in our own country. And the company that had the good luck to be "selected" to do the job had done a pitiful job with inferior materials. The walls started falling down. It just didn't make sense – all the guys were bitching about it. And where were the funds for the armored vests that the fighting men needed?

He also hadn't understood how it was possible that'd he'd only lost a leg while two of his best buddies, right next to him, lost their lives when that bomb went off. God had saved him for something. Those guys had families that needed them. When he was out-processed, Ezra chose to move, bag and baggage, back down south to his roots.

So here he was, Ezra Overmeyer, Irma Jean's and Jonathan's daddy, cruising down the highway just over the speed limit. God knows he isn't about to break any speed laws 'cause he sure doesn't want nor can afford a ticket. The highway is prime. Louisiana – competing with Mississippi, Alabama, and Tennessee – may not yet have the brass ring, but it was getting close before the Katrina debacle.

As he crossed the Pearl River – the border between Louisiana and Mississippi – he calculated he had another forty miles to go before reaching his destination, the White Sands Communities in the small town of Poplarville, Mississippi. A lot of oil wells there.

Ezra is now what his grandfather called an oil spotter – an old-fashioned term for a geologist. He's employed by the same company his daddy worked for his whole life before he cashed in his chips six months ago from lung cancer. Died in the Covington Parish Hospital, right in Ezra's arms. His dad'd been a tobacco chewer and a smoker all his life, right down to his last breath – saw no cause to change.

Ezra's company is one of the biggest seismograph companies in all of five states. And Ezra's now one of their key assets.

The White Sands Oil Wells are primarily owned by the black community – not all, but most. Inherited land, over generations, and the pump-jacks teetered their dance to bring lots of oil to the surface. Mr. Ezra Overmeyer is one of that community's favorite people. They look forward to his coming to town because he is the man who can, truly, tell them where the oil, if there is any, is located. Ninety-nine out of a hundred times. He was that good.

It was hot as hell, around three in the afternoon, when he noticed several groups of guys cornering off by themselves from time to time, complete with worried looks and hushed tones. He didn't pay it much mind until Thomas Brown, a nice guy and one of the owners of a new well, came over.

"How you doing, Mr. Overmeyer? Been hearing any of this stuff about all what's going on over there in Washington Parish?" Brown asked in a low, still voice.

Ezra pulled off his hard hat and wiped his brow with his kerchief. "Doing fine, Brown, and by the looks of you, well, I'd say you are too." He laughed and matched Thomas' serious tone when he continued, "But I don't have any idea what stuff you're talking about in Washington Parish."

Brown took a deep breath, a troubled sigh escaping before he hesitantly replied, "It's bad, sir. Over there. Real bad."

It didn't take more than ten minutes for Overmeyer to get the gist of what was going on. This young white couple had been out celebrating the night before – dancing and drinking a little too much. They had picked up their three-year-old daughter from the grandmother's house on the way home. Apparently affected by the alcohol, the husband ran off the road and mired a rear wheel in a swampy hole. Stuck, he told his wife to lock the doors and stay put, and he left on foot to get help. While he was gone, two black soldiers drove past on their way to town. A short time later, one of the soldiers – the passenger – decided to go back and check things out.

The husband returned with help to find his car's window smashed in and his wife outside the car, walking along the highway, tightly holding her daughter's hand as the young girl struggled to keep up. Both were crying. Long story short, the wife told how the black soldier had broken the window and made them get out of the car. Now this soldier, accused of assault and suspicion of rape, was being held just across the state line in Washington Parish.

Evidently, the other black soldier – the driver – was picked up and under questioning, made some pretty horrific statements, admitting to a host of crimes. Now Klan was gathering, bound and determined to enforce their brand of justice. Brown explained he and some of his fellow black cohorts were getting together, complete with their guns, for a trip to Washington Parish to head off a lynching.

Ezra took off like a bat out of hell for the parish seat. "This could end up being one helluva ugly situation," he thought. By God, it was 2008. Some of his buddies were still fighting in Iraq, and he wasn't going to stand by and see something crazy like this transpire in his own home state. "Oh, sweet Jesus!" he thought. "How in God's name can we broker peace in another country, with another culture, when we can't even get along with our own neighbor?"

The Ku Klux Klan wasn't what it used to be, thank God. Ezra's father had been a Klansman in the old days. He remembered huge fights between his parents when he was a kid, his mama almost divorcing his daddy because of a different point of view on the Klan.

But that's not to say they weren't still around. For instance, up until recently, they had a huge camp in Saucier, Mississippi, over in Harrison County. They had a Confederate flag big as a boxcar out front so people would know where to find it. They had souvenir shops and made a fortune off memorabilia, especially popular with tourists from up north.

But their Grand Marshall was busted for drugs, the property seized, and he'd been locked up in Parchman State Penitentiary in Sunflower County. He'll be there for a long, long time to come. Last spring a smaller group, led by Mississippi's Grand Dragon Douglas Cohen, in full Klan regalia – white robes, hoods, and pointed hats – surrounded the Poplarville Courthouse, protesting child abuse, domestic violence, and the prayer ban in schools and sporting events.

Just over an hour on the road, Ezra circled the Washington Parish town square park, noting cars were already parking a line-up along the streets. The commotion had started.

Ezra walked into the small jail adjacent to the courthouse. He was shocked to discover the sheriff sitting at his desk all alone. "Where're your deputies, Sheriff?"

The sheriff looked up at him doing a slow burn and said, "I ain't got any got-damned deputies. The lilly-livered, yellow-bellied cowards quit on me."

Looking around the three-celled jailhouse, Ezra spied the lone black soldier at the center of this calamity. He sat on a cot in the first cell, bent-shouldered, with despair oozing from every pore in his body. He then saw a ten foot alligator in the third cell. He got the picture real fast. The old Louisiana jail game.

Ezra spun on the sheriff. "You son-of-a-bitch!" he exclaimed, his anger burning through clenched teeth.

"Now I didn't do it!" the sheriff yelled as he got to his feet.

"You put the driver of that car last night in that cell," Ezra shouted, pointing at the cell that held the gator. "He gave this fella up in a New York minute!" he continued, nodding toward the prisoner. "In that cell with that gator he said every damn thing you wanted him to. Hell, man, you put me in a cell with a damn gator and I'd say my mother was an alien and my father was a monkey!" He paused as he looked around the meager jail, then bellowed, "Are you people crazy? No wonder wild stories and rumors are flying everywhere!" Ezra felt his face burning red with an anger he'd not known in quite a while.

The sheriff shook his head. "To hell with it all. I ain't never killed nobody in my whole life in this damn job, and I ain't about to start now."

He removed his badge and tossed it on his desk. It rung with a tone of fine metal and finality.

"What do you think you're doing?" Ezra demanded. He looked at the sheriff incredulously, wondering if the man had lost his marbles.

"I'm quitting, that's what I'm doing! And you and nobody on this God's green planet is gonna stop me."

Ezra couldn't believe it. He stood with his mouth agape. "You can't just walk out of here! Who's going to protect the prisoner?"

"I don't give a shit!" He sneered as he turned to the door and continued, "Hey, big mouth, what about you?"

He picked up one of the shiny brass stars from the six or seven piled on his desk and tossed it to Ezra. "Here. My last official act as sheriff. I hereby deputize you."

The man laid his shotgun across the desk, grabbed his hat and without further comment, walked out, slamming the door behind him.

Stunned, Ezra looked at the prisoner. The prisoner looked at him. Ezra walked over to the desk and picked up the shotgun, checking to make sure it was good to go.

That was three hours ago. Ezra had some time to organize his thoughts. He sat in a small, straight-backed chair, the gun across his lap, in the prisoner's locked cell. The keys in his pocket. The prisoner sat behind him, wide-eyed. Some could say Ezra was taking a chance, the prisoner could've jumped him. But then, who would stand between the prisoner and the enemy?

They'd had time to talk, and of course, the truth – and Ezra believed it – was far different than the lurid allegations. When his buddy had driven by, the soldier noticed the car's back wheels in the water with the woman and child inside and he was concerned for their safety. His buddy wanted nothing to do with stopping, so when he got to his car, he drove back.

Sure enough, the wheels had sunk further into the slime, the car looked like it was sinking fast, the passengers in serious danger. The husband had locked his family inside and had taken the keys. The sobbing woman was terrified. She couldn't get the electric windows down nor would she open the door. Using a rock, the soldier busted open the window, opened the door, and urged the disheveled lady and her child out. She wouldn't get into his automobile, so he used his own blanket to protect them from the chilly night air. He offered to call her husband on the cell phone, but her husband didn't have one. He suggested he call the police but she begged him not to, probably because both she and the husband had too much to drink.

"He's gonna be mad at me," she kept whimpering over and over, just like a scared kitten. "'Cause I didn't stay in the car like he tol' me."

"Ma'am, that car's in trouble. If it slid further down in there, you and your daughter could've been trapped and…"

Her body trembled as she whined on, fearful. She begged him, "Please go. You've been so kind, and I don't want any trouble!" It was as if she hadn't heard a word he said.

Even though he didn't like leaving the lady and her child alone, he knew the vibes weren't right. The soldier had strong suspicions her angry husband could prove abusive. Next thing he knows, a cop car pulled up to his home and he was whisked back across the state line to this jail, where he discovered his buddy in the next cell.

While he couldn't see his buddy from his cell, he could hear some men telling his buddy what they'd thought happened and his buddy was screaming his head off like he had a hot poker in his side. He screamed that the men were right and begged them to stop.

Ezra well understood. When he was a kid he'd heard men talking, more than once, about the Louisiana game, using a gator to get a confession. He wondered how many men, white, black, red, and yellow – innocent, but scared of alligators – were behind bars.

Ezra was no fool – he was a realist. His brow was soaked with nervous sweat, wondering how in God's name he'd gotten in this fix. He felt like Gary Cooper in that old movie, *High Noon.*

They could hear a lot of people coming up the street, mobbing around the door to see the prisoner and watch the fireworks. Ezra tensed as he heard the door handle rattle, then turn. He watched the jail door swing open as four men stepped in, decked out in full Klan ceremonial dress – white robes, masks, and pointy hats. "What in the hell do we have here?" the leader asked. He started to laugh and his buddies joined in.

"Lord God, is there one prisoner or two? I see two, what choo see?" the one to his left asked, his best stab at what he considered jovial tomfoolery. Whispered questions, comments and some titters ran through the crowd just outside the door. A few began to taunt and jeer support. A genuine mob!

"Well now," the leader sighed. He addressed Ezra. "C'mon, boy, you just put that gun down, unlock that cell, and turn that soldier out to us. We don't want no trouble."

"Uh-huh," Ezra replied calmly. "And then what?"

"And then, we take care of 'im."

"Meaning what?" Ezra pushed on. He could see the leader's eyes through the slits in the white mask. He could see them narrow.

"Listen son, that man there, wearing a soldier's uniform, raped a white woman early this morning, not far from here and…"

Ezra interrupted, "Why don't you just say, 'raped a woman?' Because it's just as bad to rape a black or yellow woman as it is a white woman."

The leader held his hand up, quieting the crowd and his voice steeled with anger. "Son, I don't have time for smart-mouthing, you hear me? We plan to take care of this problem right now. That prisoner you sitting in front of raped a woman and we can't have something happening like *this* in our county!"

He could hear the soldier's anxiety rising as he drew a deep breath.

Ezra slowly shook his head, "No, we sure can't."

"Glad you see the light. Now, turn 'im over."

Sucking in his bottom lip, Ezra spoke in a very quiet but commanding voice, "Take the sheet off, Herman." Ezra, as luck would have it, recognized the voice and the man from when he was a kid. He hadn't particularly liked him then, either.

The man laughed. "That's old Overmeyer's son? His daddy was a good man." Herman, in his late seventies, slowly pulled the hood away from his head. "Now you be a good boy and behave 'for you get yoahself in some bad trouble."

"You listen to me, this man didn't rape anybody. I know."

One of the other men draped in a Klan outfit snarled, "What in the hell gives you the right to think you *know*?"

Ezra stood up, tall in the momentary silence, broken only by the click of the cocked hammer being uncocked – the double-barrel shotgun still not moving. Slowly Ezra lowered it to his side, but held it close.

"What this soldier did is not for you to decide, no more than the pilots who crashed those jets into New York's Twin Towers had *any right* to make that decision!" Ezra cleared his throat. "You realize, Herman, we haven't had a lynching in the south in over half a century. Oh, I know, you didn't ever really hang people, not hang 'em on a tree. Uh-uh. You just put a rope around their neck and pulled 'em up on their tippy toes just enough so they wouldn't choke. They'd stand for hours until they were so exhausted they dropped, hanging themselves. Lets you off the hook, ya think?"

Ezra sadly shook his head and continued. "I just got back less than a year ago from Iraq, fighting against terrorists – for your country – and now, I want you," and Ezra, taking a deep breath suddenly raised the shotgun and pointed it at them. He spoke in a low, even tone, "To take off those goddamn white sheets! I don't care if it's a black hood covering a terrorist face, or a white hood covering your cowardly faces in the name of freedom, I don't like it."

Ezra's voice escalated with pent-up anger, rising and octave or two as he continued, "Or my country torturing men at Abu Gharib in Iraq, or our people water-boarding prisoners at Gitmo, it's all the same fucking thing – WRONG – and I'm sick to death of it!

"Remember, I have been trained to kill, so if you want to take him, then you do it over my dead body!

"And, by the way, then you can ask him yourself if he did it. Ask him when you're all on the other side. And you'll be able to do that because by-god in heaven, I promise you, you'll be dead too!"

The soldier rode with Ezra the eighty miles back to New Orleans, then on across the causeway to a nearby parish's sheriff. The soldier's cousin, a lawyer, met up with them. They filed a complete report and as a protective measure, secured a restraining order against the four men for "Intended Assault."

On his ride home Ezra thought again about wars. "My God, there were so many. Look at World War II," he reminded himself. "More than 50 million people killed, some say as many as 70 million. Unbelievable.

And as if that wasn't enough, then came Korea, Vietnam, Cambodia, the Gulf, and on and on. But the worst wars of all," he considered, "are the little wars inside each one of us."

It was almost eleven that night. With any luck he'd be in bed before midnight, hugging his pretty wife. A quick stop at Walgreens to pick up three cute stuffed animals. There was the white fluffy teddy bear with a red heart for Essie, a kitty with a crown on her head, holding a pink pocket book with a dollar for Irma Jean, and a monkey holding a soccer ball for Jonathan.

"You gotta love life, he smiled to himself, "as long as you're lucky enough to be in life."

The Chicken Coop

The skinny blonde tilted her head back, befitting the budding teenager's anger. Flicking her eyelashes, she tried to hide the tear rising filling her vision as she pulled the wire tightly around the chicken coop.

"I don't care," Moment mumbled. "You always do that."

"What?" her father replied in a loud, harsh voice.

"Scream for me to come out here and help you, just as I'm puttin' the meringue on my lemon pie." Her lip trembled with a pout.

"I don't care about any damn lemon pie, girl. I need help, now. And when I say 'now' I mean *now*, not tomorrow."

Preston thought to himself, "Why do I have to sound so mean?" Glancing at his only child, his sweet daughter, he thought, "Maybe I'm angry 'cause I'm losing my little tomboy."

Little Moment had been dubbed with the nickname "Olive Oyl," after *Popeye*'s skinny cartoon girlfriend. But this child was beginning to blossom – quickly now that she was a freshman in high school.

Cognizant of the changes, dreading the fact that his precious little girl is growing up, he thought to himself, "Time, hell, when you want it to hurry up, you have to wait. And when you beg it to slow down, the sucker just goes too fast. Too damn fast!"

Then he continued, only instead of speaking, he sang in a rhyme, that handle he used to make light of all situations.

"*If you wait until tomorrow, then girl, I'll be filled with sorrrrrrrooow*,"

It was his way of making peace.

Opening the door of the old bright blue Chevrolet, he began loading up the boxes of poultry products – powder was the chicken medicine – placing them in the back seat. Better than good was the medicine, producing important cures for poultry and livestock diseases – for cholera, roup, sorehead, and white diarrhea, and consistently resulting in better egg production, even during molting season.

"Mighty fine products. Best in Mississippi – hell, best anywhere!" Preston told himself proudly. Spittin' the cigar's chewed tobacco back to mother earth, he muttered to himself, "Those damn professional feed companies have a racket, ripping off poor people, sidewinding 'em with overpriced products, making deals to take a percent of everything farmers own, just for a few bucks of stuff. What a slick and pitiful way to do business." He shook his head. "Guess they think the little people should just go suck an egg."

Farmers need to keep every dime they can get their hands on. They have to get their kids' teeth fixed just like everybody else. Preston Taylor's own daddy had been a farmer. Nobody had it harder. They were lucky, most of the time – had food on the table even if it was just grits with sorghum. Some didn't. A box of Taylor's powder cost only one dollar and can cure fifty chickens of white diarrhea. The feed companies would take fifteen dollars to do the same thing. But then, as Preston always had always tried to comprehend, "I guess that's the darn reality of Big Business."

Preston looked at his daughter, who was watching a grasshopper trying to jump from a rock onto a rose.

He laughed, "C'mon, baby, Grandma was slow, but, honey, she was old!"

"Sureeeeee," Moment nodded. "Puttin' me down cause I'm in there cookin' instead of helpin' you. Isn't my fault you didn't have no son. You should've adopted one!"

"I ain't raisin' nobody else's young-uns but my own," he replied stubbornly for the thousandth time.

"You're the first one in the kitchen to eat the pie," she shook her head.

"Well, now ain't that the truth," he laughed. "Why don't you go finish it so I can have some lemon pie for breakfast." He smacked his lips teasingly. "And I'll load up the rest. You and yoah mama hurry up that lunch for the road, too, girl. The sun's coming up. I don't want you and me to be late getting out of heah!" he yelled at the back of her head as she flew up the stairs of the little white suburban house trimmed in blue. The front of the house bespoke her mother's soft delicate hand, charmingly inviting, with an assortment of potted plants and pastel flowers adorning the little porch, and the old swing with its new coat of fresh white paint.

The backyard bespoke her daddy's existence. It served as a fenced in home for his four birddogs, Luellen Setters, the finest in the country. Next to the fence sat the large wooden box used to mix up the Taylor Poultry Products and right beside it, the huge black cauldron for concocting the worming liquid – for dogs, cows, and pigs – terrific products. But the ugly cauldron, sitting right there in the middle of the neighborhood, was an embarrassment for the moment. Scurrying through the living room, her long legs covering the small space in a matter of seconds, she called out, "Momma, Daddy's ready to go."'

Smiling proudly, Moment carefully extracted her treasures from the second-hand stove, and setting the two pies with their lightly browned meringue curlicues on the sink shelf for cooling, she nodded. They'd be perfect by the time she got back home.

Moment walked outside and tucked the brown paper lunch bags that her Momma had prepared behind the seat of the car. The aroma of fried chicken whet her appetite even though she was already full.

She knew Momma had also tucked in hunks of cheese and hard boiled eggs along with the biscuits, but the heavenly thing was that there would always be a piece of cake. As she waited for her daddy to yell out, "Let's go," her eyes moved past the fence to the huge old wooden crates that held the ingredients used to mix up the medicines he sold wholesale and retail.

Entering her adolescent years, Moment'd become more aware of a dividing world. Kids who'd been best friends as children had begun to split into class groups as awareness of the divisions their parents had set up before them stepped up to plate. And, of course, they fell into line. Moment didn't understand why everybody couldn't belong to each other. But she guessed the truth was they didn't really want to. She was a middle-of-the-roader, caught between her friends whose parents sold hot dogs at the drive-in theater, and the country club set.

The Country Club had invited Preston to join. It didn't cost but a little bit of money. Moment was real excited about it because then she could learn to play golf and some of those fancy things her daddy referred to as high-falutin' and just didn't seem to care about. A lot of the men were rich, but they really liked Taylor and so, they had asked him to join. But he wouldn't do it! And it made her so mad. She'd asked him why.

"No," he said. "I guess I couldn't keep the kinda friends I like if I joined."

"Why not? What do you mean?"

"Well, my friends like Chicken and Big Boy."

"Well now, I know they aren't going to ask Chicken and Big Boy to join the Country Club!"

"That's not what I mean," he replied. "I just don't want to be around somebody that might look down on them."

The men were two guys who went hunting a lot with Preston. Chicken raised the most beautiful pointer bird dogs you ever saw. He was nicknamed Chicken because he looked just like a chicken. He only had one ear and Moment couldn't figure out if he was born that way or if somebody cut it off. She used to try to peek at it when he came over, but he'd always catch her and she'd quickly look the other way, embarrassed.

Big Boy was a nice guy, real sweet 'til he got drunk. Then he became a kleptomaniac. Well, he didn't steal valuable things but he just *had* to steal. He'd usually come in the house and look around, then steal something – like a steak. He'd put it under his coat and walk out. That was the thrill of his life.

"Like I said, Daddy, I know the Country Club isn't gonna ask Chicken or Big Boy to join!"

Moment had to help her daddy mix the powder and the liquid potions brewing in the humongous black cauldron. She hated it because he'd run around the house wearing a ripped-up shirt and old pants that he'd torn off at the knee, an ole hat, and he had chalk-colored powder all over him, stinking up the whole neighborhood. Then, after it was all mixed, the teenager always wanted to go to the library or head downtown with one of her girlfriends, even if all they did was sit and study people as they'd pass by.

But then, she couldn't, because they had to make starch in the huge pot. They'd take toothbrushes, and using them carefully, spread starch on labels and lids. Following that, they had to roll the labels onto the bottles and boxes.

Preston had received an abundance of letters from businessmen and agricultural colleges, raving about the results that had been obtained while using his products. However, Taylor was content with his world as it was. He made enough money to pay the bills and then took off and went fishing. And busied himself writing songs for his friends and singin' 'em.

The young girl's thoughts turned to her junior sorority group whose meeting she'd miss that evening. They met every two weeks in their organdy or taffeta dresses and white gloves for a young ladies' Southern get-together, sipping tea and pretending they were Scarlet O'Hara while discussing boys and life.

Moment had a few little qualms about her fellow sorority members. At the last meeting, it seemed they spent the whole time gossiping about one of their older members – a sixteen-year-old girl who was PREGNANT! The girl's father, a very rich doctor, was shipping his daughter out of state so nobody would know. They all knew. The tearful girl had shared with her best friend that her father, instead of offering compassion, had belittled his daughter with one devastating comment: "We're appalled. You certainly haven't conducted yourself, in any manner whatsoever, like the little *lady* we've raised!"

The girl, a sweet little thing, was broken-hearted. She loved her boyfriend, but her daddy had threatened to kill him and was going to make her give the baby to an orphanage. While a lot of the girls tittered, Moment thought it was all so awfully messed up and sad. It would be years before the twelve-year-old might learn that "lady" is a four-letter word and can sometimes be used as a game. And that the word "woman" might be more important. Moment was feeling remorseful because she'd missed the opportunity – too embarrassed – to speak up in defense of the young pregnant girl at the meeting. It was important to her, as it is to all of us seeking approval, wanting to belong, and to be accepted by our friends and peers.

Moment didn't always have an easy time with her classmates. Like when on Sunday, at church, her daddy had been too tired to remove the chicken coop from the back of the car and insisted on driving his automobile, with the feathers still clinging to it, right up in front of the door. She felt the shame creep up her neck as she listened to the giggles of the other kids.

As her daddy finished packing the last box of chicken medicine into the car, she was brought back to the moment by his voice. "Moment," he yelled. "Let's hit the road!"

The girl was fascinated as always by the magnificent soft changes of vibrant color and graceful beauty as dawn's fingers rippled into the early morning sky. As Preston drove, he waved at a passing stranger. Meridian, Mississippi was a friendly little city and one didn't pass another human on the road without some sort of communication. Taylor always said, "Hell, even dogs sniff each other. Human beings, if they got the brains God gave 'em, ought to at least smile at each other while they have a chance." Meridian, population 60,000, was big enough to have some privacy, yet small enough for smiles.

After a while, she and her father began to sing. Preston's bass voice boomed *Swing Low, Sweet Chariot* throughout the car as Moment accompanied him in her light lilting voice, their acappella some form of harmony. Later, as the highway unfolded beneath them, they played games to pass the time.

First, they'd play "cowpoker." He'd count the cows on his side of the car and Moment would count her side. Whoever got the most cows collected a penny a head. Her father usually lost. He said, "Because I have to watch the road." But, Moment often wondered if he'd let her win. Then, they'd name the different kinds of trees that flew past – oak pine, elm, cedar, sycamore. Her father taught her many things that did not apply to the society in which they lived. They were lessons in knowledge that shed wisdom – lessons that warmed her heart, such as how to find your way out of the woods by looking at the stars. Her daddy knew a lot of things that men who had finer educations would never know.

Leaving the highway, they tread the back roads, as he wanted to sell a few boxes of chicken medicine along the way. He sold wholesale and retail, door-to-door, throughout the whole state of Mississippi, and, on occasion, parts of Alabama, Louisiana, Arkansas, Georgia, Florida, and even Texas. It was with pride that she watched people greet him from doors, cars, and fields. "Hey, Taylor!" Always making her feel that her daddy was a loved man and that she, his daughter, must also be loved 'cause she was part of him.

People always welcomed him, insisting they sit down and have something to eat. There was always plenty of creamed corn, fresh cake, dumplings – whatever was on the stove. But then there were some houses where there was absolutely nothing to eat. One time they'd come across this Indian family cooking grass because they were starving. Her daddy'd given 'em some money to buy food – his profits for the day.

They came across people who didn't even know what a radio was and children who didn't own one single, solitary pair of shoes. Moment and her mother always packed up any clothes or anything else in the house that wasn't being used to give to somebody who needed it. Sometimes Preston would smile – sometimes he'd get mad.

"You women can throw it out faster with a spoon than I can bring it in with a shovel! You'll give away every darn thing I have if I don't watch you!"

After a number of selling stops, Preston smiled mischievously. "Hey, Moment, you want to try a few houses?" On occasion, at her request, he'd let her try her hand. Pretending to be older, she'd deliver the sales pitch with conviction and did quite well, earning a whole fifty cents on each box.

"Sure," she replied quickly, proud of the chance to prove herself, but noting an odd tone to his voice.

"I'll bet you five dollars you can't sell the next house," he smirked.

"What's the matter?" she inquired. "The next house doesn't have any chickens?"

"God, girl, you are suspicious. I just thought I'd let you earn a little bit of money, but I just thought maybe you weren't in the mood and I bet you couldn't get with it, that's all!"

"O.K.," she replied, examining his smile. "I'll take the bet."

Her arms loaded with boxes and bottles, she tentatively knocked on the large weather-worn door of the old wooden framed house. A soft-smiling but very elderly woman answered, and was soon joined by another lovely silver-haired elderly lady. When Moment inquired, "Are you the boss of the chickens?" the lady smiled sweetly.

"Well, ma'am," Moment continued. "I'm Dr. Preston Taylor's daughter and we've got the best medicine in the country, which you probably know."

The lady again smiled sweetly.

"It's for cholera, roup, sorehead, white diarrhea, as well as insured egg production, even during molting season. And we've got…" Moment continued a ten-minute sales pitch, just as her daddy had taught her. When she got all through and out of breath, she asked for the sale and waited patiently for a response.

"What's that she says?" the lady's companion yelled in a quivery voice.

"I don't know, I couldn't hear 'er!" replied the boss of the chickens.

Moment stood there shocked with the realization that the two old ladies were almost stone deaf. In her mind's ear, she could hear her daddy's laughter all the way across the road.

Approaching the car, Moment sidled up to the window. Preston was laughing. "You didn't ask me if they could hear," he said, throwing his hands up in the air.

"That's O.K. Daddy," she replied hoarsely as she victoriously pulled a struggling chicken out from behind her back. They didn't have a dollar, the price of the powder per box, so she'd traded for a chicken – exactly what her Daddy'd do. That was the part she hated, catching the chickens he would sometimes trade for. Her daddy would take them into town and sell. She was afraid they'd peck 'er – and they usually did.

As she basked in winning the bet, they meandered along the

highway coming across a large group of dusty, tired-looking men alongside the road, wearing black and white striped uniforms. They were shackled together with large black chains and being guarded by police troopers with guns.

"Daddy!" she exclaimed in shock. "What are those men doing?"

"They're working the fields," he replied. "They're criminals, honey. They're being punished and taught their lessons to be made fit for society."

She thought about it for awhile, studying the freedom of the birds and feeling the wind whipping through the window against her face. She pondered, "Daddy, how can you teach a man to be a human being if you're treating him worse than a poor ole' dog?"

He nodded his head, not answering, but amazed at her grasp of humanity.

They stopped for lunch at a little country store and had crackers, cheese and a bottle of Orange Crush, saving her Mother's packed chicken for later, in case it got past supper before they returned. Afterwards, Moment watched the hills as the fields unfold past their car, mesmerized by the raw beauty of the rural landscape.

Preston pulled the now dusty automobile alongside the thick brush on the deserted country gravel road.

"Time for a break," he smiled.

Tired from driving, he stretched his arms far right and then left. Moment, having anticipated the direction they were heading, peeled off her clothes to reveal the bathing suit underneath. Preston led the way to one of the many swimming holes he knew, warning the girl as they went along to be sure and follow directly in his path, watching out for poison ivy, snakes, and spiders.

A few lazy trout darted curiously underneath the smooth surface as it reflected the crystalline blue from heaven's vault. As she slipped into the water, her body thrilled to the pond's cool velvety fingers swirling around her.

Looking up she wondered to herself, "Where is God today?"

"Everywhere," the nuns had said.

"Probably true," she thought to herself as she sighed, staring at the vastness of the horizon.

Moment and her mother were two of the handful of Catholics in Meridian. In fact, there were hardly any Catholics in Mississippi. Only seven kids in her class, and two were Jewish! The Catholics and the Jews hung out together. Of course, Sister Mary Gertrude said, "That's the way it's supposed to be because Jesus was Jewish!"

Daddy was a hard-shell Baptist. At least, that was supposedly how he was raised according to his family – and most were Baptist. But Daddy said that he never even got baptized! On the day he was supposed to be dunked, the preacher ran off with another man's wife! Grandma Haittie never wanted to hear this story. Even so, Daddy liked to go to Mass with Momma on Sunday, even if it was just to sleep.

Monsignor Burns always said that it was good to hang out with atheists, actually. "Because," he said, "God walks behind the religious man, at the side of the agnostic, but sits right on the shoulder of the atheist, riding herd. So when you're with an atheist, you're in good company!"

"Daddy," Moment shook her head spraying drops of water, shattering the mirror surface. "Is that true when you were a little boy you ran when you saw a priest?"

"Yes, ma'am," he smiled, sitting on the small bank, warming himself in the golden violet rays of the late afternoon sun. "I'd run like all get out!"

Preston moved his tongue against his bottom lip and sucked in his top lip against his teeth, remembering his childhood. "Well, you know," he continued by way of explanation, "The priests wear black, so you can't always see 'em at night, and they could make you disappear into the night."

"Good Gawd, Daddy!" she interrupted.

"Don't cuss," he reprimanded her.

"Do you mean to tell me that there's some grown-ups that still believe that?"

"Yep, 'fraid so, honey," he replied, remembering yesteryear nervously.

Preston looked up at the sky, concerned as he checked for any telltale signs of rain. Rising up, he turned and started through the woods. "Let's go, Baby."

They'd traveled about one-hundred-and-fifty miles that day when the clouds engulfed them. By late afternoon they were caught in a serious thunderstorm. Lightning was flashing all around and suddenly struck right next to the car.

"Oh, ho," her daddy exclaimed with concern. He'd always had a fear of lightning, ever since he was a kid and his bird-dog Princess had been killed by it. "That's it. We're not going on any more tonight."

He stared ahead at the old house in the distance. It was the only one around.

"Oh, boy," he muttered to himself, "Damn! Oh, s'cuse me, honey," he nodded to his daughter. "I didn't mean to say that. I'd sure rather not stay there. I don't like the woman who lives there," Preston shook his head. "But the storm's too bad to go on any further," he sighed.

The sixty-seven-year-old country woman was big, with stern face and manner.

"But, hey, she seems alright," Moment thought.

"Where's your niece?" Preston inquired of the woman.

An odd expression spread across her face. Getting up and slipping into an old black raincoat and boots, the woman replied, "She's gone out to the barn – guess most likely, she's caught out there in the rain."

Without another word, she grabbed an umbrella and headed out the back door.

Now this storm had been going on for some time. Moment, whose common sense wasn't limited by her youth, felt it unusually odd that the woman had waited this long to go out there and see about the girl.

Soon enough, the woman came scrambling back with this tall, scared ten-year-old girl in tow, clad only in a worn cotton dress, the wet fabric clinging to her thin, angular frame. The child wasn't even wearing a sweater and it had turned real cold. Moment tried to be friendly with the poor ole girl but she appeared too frightened to even look at her.

Later, the house had gone to sleep. Moment didn't know what time it was when she first heard the anguished cries. Sitting bolt upright in bed, she felt her heart pounding with a terrifying fear. Curiosity, dominant in her nature, got the better of her and slipping out of bed, she tiptoed down the hall, her ears and instinct leading the way. Scary moans and pathetic whimpers were emanating from the child's room.

The echo of heavy footsteps sent a warning through Moment's bones and she instantly withdrew into a safe hiding nook behind the bathroom door, across from the girl's room. Moment's pulse raced as she strained to listen.

She had never, in her whole life, heard such a wallop! The woman hissed loudly. "You wake up and shut up!" She must have slapped that girl clean out of bed.

Moment, with eerie chills running up and down her spine, crept into her daddy's room as fast as she could. He wasn't asleep.

"Go back to bed, honey," Preston said as he gave his daughter a comforting hug. "The girl's probably being punished for something."

"Ohhhh, Daddy," she stuttered and she thought to herself, "I'll just bet!"

"I'll check it in the morning, Honey. I give you my word, Sugah. Now, you get some sleep, you heah."

The dawn had not yet wakened from its divine sojourn when her daddy's flashlight pierced her dream. He simply said, "Get dressed, now."

She was up like a flash and dressed in two minutes. When Moment got downstairs the woman was up, asking, "You folks sure you don't want any breakfast? My lord, I got bacon, biscuits and gravy, fresh eggs..."

'Nooooo," Preston interrupted. "Thank you very much," he mumbled, and continued, "Gotta get on the road. Long way to go."

Soon, Preston was doing some tall driving.

After ten minutes, Moment asked in a small voice, "What's up?"

"Not much," he replied nervously, his mouth tight, eyes glued to the highway.

When they got to the sheriff's office, Preston tried to be real calm.

"I don't know what to make of this, but I thought I'd better speak to you about it."

Preston explained the events of the evening before, repeating that he'd never liked that old woman.

"Well, I couldn't go back to sleep. I just lay there," he told the sheriff. "Finally, I figured I may as well get up, check the car and everything. Part of my chicken coop was loosened by the wind, and I was trying to find a piece of wire to fix it. Went around to the backyard and noticed that the storm shelter door was open.

"Well," he continued, "I was going to close it when I saw this huge heavy chain. It was attached to this large ol' stake nailed in the ground. On the other end was tied a piece of rope. And there was a leather strap, you know, the kind for shuffling animals in a chute, and a tin bowl with some water in it, like for a dog. Could've been there for years, I don't know, but you see, there was another dish with a big hunk of bread and some sloppy food in it, and the stuff was fresh. And, you know," Preston tried to cover with a nervous laugh, "I'll tell ya," he cleared his throat.

"You see, *she don't have no dog!"*

The sheriff said he'd had another call about that woman not too long back. "Some schoolgirl saw some pretty bad bruises on this woman's niece."

Preston had to sign an official complaint and the sheriff took off.

Heading back home, Preston said in a shaky voice, "It'd be best not to tell Mother 'bout what'd happened, 'cause, it would only serve to depress 'er."

Later that night, the sheriff called.

"Mr. Taylor, I gotta thank you. We should've followed up on this, hell, a long time ago. Seems this ole woman's sister had done run off and eloped with the man she loved! Uh huh, can you believe it? That's right. Then, to add insult, in her mind, to injury, her sister gave birth to this darling little baby girl. Her niece. Unfortunately, as the fates would have it, both parents were killed in an automobile accident when this child was only four years old, and this woman, the only relative, was given control and supervision to raise this young'un! As it turns out, horrible mistake! Damn, she's been taking all her stored-up hate out on this child ever since. This kid was suffering from malnutrition and she was really beat up, even had a broken rib!"

"Jesus H!" Preston shook his head sadly and hung up the phone. Turning to his own child he stated in a quiet voice, "You know, Baby, I don't like poking my nose in other people's business but, my God, don't ever forget, you can't turn your back on somethin' like that!"

Sighing from the heaviness of the day and taking a load off his feet, he sat down on Tippy Jo's organdy ruffled bedcover as his gaze appreciated every detail of the dainty, feminine little room. He studied his daughter, whom he loved so much. He wondered how could anybody treat a child like that. My God, suppose he and his wife had been killed in an accident – who knows who would have gotten custody of his kid? It could happen to anybody.

Moment was sitting on the floor beside the foot of the bed, busily reorganizing her cedar hope chest. Placing within the hope chest the pink and white quilt, a gift from Taylor's sister, her Aunt Jonnie B., Moment looked up at her daddy, the unasked question in her penetrating dark brown inquiring eyes: "Why?"

It was time for Preston, with help from his angels, to try and give some kind of answer.

"Well," he smiled. "Sugah, in EVERY problem there's a gift, but you HAVE to look for it, and, here it is – a lesson. God gave us two ears to hear twice; two eyes to see twice; two nostrils to breathe twice; and one mouth to speak once. And if somebody is mean as hell or acts like a fool, don't get down on their level cause then you're a fool, too. And if somebody thinks you are a fool, you look twice, listen twice and shut your mouth once and for all. So you don't give 'em the chance to prove themselves right!"

"Why, Daddy," she laughed through the day's sadness, "I didn't know you were a philosopher!"

"Hey." He got up and trying to lift them both out of the memory of that tragic experience, he tried to laugh as he juked out of the room. "There's a lot about yoah ole Dad you don't know. There's a lot about everything, honey, we all don't know.

"Guess, I gotta go find me a new piece of chicken wire." And giving a little wave to his treasure and closed the door.

The Orange Jacket

"Hit 'im in the neck." Lee angrily spat the words out through gritted teeth.

"Whare?" Astride the kid, Duffy pulled back his blood-smeared fist, and awkwardly turning his head, looked up askew at Lee.

Shifting from one foot to the other, Lee snarled, "Aw, hell. You ain't a damn bit of good in a stomp! Let's go."

Duffy, looking back down at the kid's face, felt a pang of useless regret as he muttered, "Jesus, I broke his nose. He's in pretty bad shape!" Lifting himself and pulling his body up, he stumbled away. "I didn't mean to…"

"Get off my damn jacket!" Lee interrupted with a yell. "You're stepping on it!" And pulling it out from underneath its owner, the loser of the fight, he almost sent Duffy tumbling.

"Your jacket?" Duffy retorted.

"Yeah." Lee slipped his arms into the sleeves and began dusting it off. "To the victor go the spoils. And anyway," he stretched his shoulders high like a proud peacock, "Orange is my favorite color. Always has been."

Wiping blood on the grass, Duffy asked himself, "What the heck? I'm a victor too – I'm the one who did the beating." But, once again, he kept his thoughts inward, never voicing them out loud – caught up in hero worship.

Lee was his God. Both were on the same football team, but Lee was the star while Duffy warmed the bench. Maybe they'd bonded because both families lived in Mississippi, right next door to Louisiana. Duffy's people were workers in the little town of Pritchett – having persevered long and hard, enabling them to send their boy to college. Lee's people lived up by Poplarville, extremely well-off, with holdings in the Mississippi pecan industry. His family had wanted him to go to his dad's alma mater, Mississippi Southern, but he'd heard that Louisiana State University was a whole heck of a lot more fun.

When the boys found themselves in fights, which happened quite often, turned out Duffy was the front man and usually did the fighting while Lee spurred him on with cusses. Duffy knew some of the other guys on their football team referred to him, behind his back, as Lee's lackey. Duffy didn't care – the rewards were plentiful – meat from the shark's mouth: attention, parties, girls, fun, and excitement. Except he did care that Lee's quick temper and harsh judgments got them into situations that he wasn't too proud of, like beating the hell out of this kid tonight.

"Why?" he pondered belatedly. "That kid really didn't do a damn thing to us. Jesus, it was a waste – totally unnecessary – just 'cause he's a little fag."

He was well aware that Lee hated queers. It was one of his things. Wiping some more blood from his chin, he thought, "Well, I guess San Francisco damn well shouldn't have been picked as the location for our team trip. Who knew?"

Interrupting his thoughts, Lee moved ahead, "Let's get the hell outta here. C'mon, boy, we gotta go places."

We must… we must…

We must increase our bust.

The bigger the better,

The tighter the sweater,

The boys are depending on us!

Lee Boudreaux could hear, in his mind's ear, the cheerleaders' chant, surprising the team with a send-off in that June heat as the plane left New Orleans for the Golden Gate City. Of the eleven main players on their team, only the families of eight boys had agreed, and could afford, the high school graduation gift – a trip to a favorite city for the boys. Most of 'em would be together in the fall: freshman at LSU. The parents thought this *gift* would be an opportunity for growth, an adventure for the young men. Seventeen-year-old Lee was going for a law degree, not because he was that ambitious, but because his uncle's firm was guaranteeing his future.

Of course they had a chaperone, but the professor, a sophisticated married man, was just now off alone, fostering the acquaintance of a pretty redhead whom he'd repeatedly met in the bar over the last few days. The boys jumped at the chance to spread their wings alone.

The streetcar heading toward Market Street clanged its signal, approaching a stop. At least Lee knew where Market Street was. He could see the magnificent Golden Gate Bridge in the distance. They'd been all over the area these last couple of days: the ferry boat run from Fisherman's Wharf over to the Islands – Sausalito, Tiburon, and a nod away, Angel Island, to bike around – hiking in the Marin headlands. They'd even gone over to beautiful Santa Cruz, swimming on those incredible beaches, surfing and fishing. Returning, they'd completed obligatory shopping from the famed Ferry Plaza at the foot of Market Street. He'd already bought souvenir presents – wines, chocolates, cheeses, and whatnots for everybody, including his old aunts and teachers. Also for his three girlfriends – each of whom prayed she was the only one. He tried to go steady with the one he liked the most, but it was just too boring, all that same female chatter over and over. Jeeze, how could anybody stand it!

None of the team had ever heard of or even known there was such a thing as "Gay Pride Day." June is the month for San Francisco's big parade, with thousands of people attending and marching. Now, here's the team right dab in the middle of it! Lee, Duffy and the rest of the guys had never seen anything like this – never been so shocked in their lives.

There were the "Wells Fargo" gays, the "Church" gays, the "Gap" gays and on and on. There were even "P Flag Marchers" – parents and friends of lesbians and gays!

There were hundreds of gay men on the street, thick as butter, four deep. In one part of the town, there were a lot of men almost nude, with their butts hanging like bait and little leather or leopard skin or something weird – cock covers and that was it! Lee and the guys thought it was disgusting. Said it made 'em sick.

Lee hated gays, alright. His daddy said they were an abomination and would burn in hell. When Lee and his teammates were playing in the lockers and around the showers, snapping each others' butts with the towels – if they seemed to be having too much fun – Coach really chastised 'em, brought 'em up straight.

One thing he liked to do this past senior year, now that he could pretend he was eighteen, he and a couple of buddies would sneak down to the French Quarter and catch a transvestite show and razz 'em. Once, they'd *caught one* afterwards, in an alley, and beat the shit out of 'im. It was one the most fun nights of Lee's memory.

"It's our stop," Duffy said, interrupting Lee's thoughts. "Why don't we head over to our hotel?"

"Heck, no!" Lee replied. "Man, it's early!"

"It's almost two in the morning, Lee."

"So? Who gives a damn? Man, the night is young!"

"But, we don't even know – where's the rest of our team?" Duffy was tired and worried and he knew that Lee had too much to drink. He didn't want any more trouble.

"Oh, bother!" Lee mocked. "You sound like Eeyore, man, that

donkey in Winnie the Pooh." He shrugged, "Either we lost them or they lost us, who cares? The night is young and so are we – this may be a once in a lifetime experience. C'mon, Dude," and pulling Duffy up he laughed, "Let's go have some fun."

The kid moaned through blurred vision as he tried to lift his head up off the concrete. Everything hurt, especially his face and one of his ribs. "God, why?" he wondered. He hadn't done anything to them – didn't even know them. Blaine tried to remember… this one guy, an incredibly handsome guy, was bragging on Blaine's new jacket, made 'im feel so good. They bought 'im a round of drinks and then later, told 'im they wanted to show 'im something outside, something special. They'd led 'im around in back and the next thing he knew he heard Lee – yeah, that was his name, Lee. In this almost happy voice, Lee said softly, "Hit 'im." Before Blaine even knew it had happened, the short guy had knocked 'im down on the ground and just started beating on 'im. He'd pleaded, begged 'em to stop – even cried, and that made the guy start beating 'im worse.

"Oh, my God, my nose!" Blaine tried to hold his face with one hand while pushing himself up with the other. He was terrified. There was blood all over 'im - his blood. He glanced around past nightly shadows to make sure they were gone. He had to get back to Ginger's house in the Mission district somehow. It was a quite a walking distance.

"I'll never make it," he muttered out loud. He checked his pockets – they hadn't even taken his wallet.

"My God, my jacket!" The realization that it was missing hit him full force. "Oh, Lord, my brand new jacket!" He sat there in pain, dumbfounded.

Blaine Logan was from Pine Bluff, Arkansas. There weren't many gays in Pine Bluff and those who were, hid it. They somehow found each other and stuck together in a non-confrontational, quiet group, trying to be invisible, not wanting to attract undesired attention – always pretending to be something they weren't.

Blaine, of slight bone and build, had just turned eighteen. His family didn't have the means to afford him a college education so he was out to get a job and make his way – and make something of himself. He was one of three children and different from the get-go. He didn't like the boys' games – too rough – he was always getting hurt. He liked to hang out with the girls, be one of them, telling stories, laughing. Wanted to help his mother sew and he was good at it, but his daddy had gotten furious and beat the hell out of 'im, more than once. He thought when he got away from there, he'd never have to take a beating again – guess he thought wrong.

His best friend was Ginger Talman, two years older than him – also from Pine Bluff and also gay – and the kindest and most caring person he'd ever known. She'd made her way to San Francisco and encouraged 'im. "C'mon, it's great, you can stay with me!" She had an apartment in the Mission District among the Hispanics. Lesbian women never had as much money as their counterparts, the gay men, so they took apartments in the less expensive Latino area.

Blaine had worked two jobs, after school, all year. He saved his money, then hopped a Greyhound out west. He'd never had pretty clothes and Ginger had helped him pick out his terrific new orange jacket. He'd fallen in love with it the minute he saw it – the nicest thing he'd ever owned – filling him with a feeling of respect. Ginger had begged him, "You got to be here for the big parade!" She'd been in the parade, one of the *Dikes on Bikes*. She'd driven one of the 450 motorcycles, women driving, sometimes two abreast. They now changed their group's title to be politically correct, to *The Women's Motorcycle Contingency*.

Blaine, arriving just a week-and-a-half earlier, expected to live like the song, *"Thank God, I'm Free."* And now, this? He'd falsely believed that kind of meanness was just in little towns like the one in which he'd been reared.

"Guess hate can pop up anywhere," he thought to himself sadly. Getting up, he figured he could get back inside, wash up and hop a bus – a short ride – home. "My nose will heal and so will my ego. I'm going to get a job – going to get myself another jacket just like the one I had, only I'm not going to follow anybody to a dark place to see something special, ever again."

A big lesson learned hard.

They looked up at the sign to see where they were – the BART station. "C'mon, man, one more stop." Lee was three sheets to the wind.

``It's three o'clock in the morning – Jesus, c'mon Lee – man, and most of the bars are closed." Duffy was falling asleep on his feet.

"Listen," Lee muttered with a laugh. "Be a good sport. Let's take one quick ride on the train, get off, have one drink and we'll cab it back to our place. I promise. It's just that, you see, I hate to give this night up."

"Alright, one more stop and that's it. But you got to promise me, no more trouble. I'm too tired – can't handle it."

Lee crossed his heart, whispering, "Cross my heart and hope to die!"

The BART train took them to the Castro Street station in a matter of minutes, and they got off. As soon as they walked up the stairs, the facts hit them right in the face. Castro Street was *the* gay district and the music from the gay clubs enveloped their senses. Nearby, there must have been at least fifty gay men, either ardently involved with their partner or giving them the once over. They seemed to be everywhere.

Looking around, Lee vaguely remembered a story about Castro Street, from way before his birth. Harvey Milk, the gay supervisor of San Francisco, also known as the Mayor of Castro Street, was murdered along with Mayor George Moscone at City Hall. The murderer had entered a plea of insanity, based on his so-called diminished capacity because of the fourteen "Twinkies" he'd just eaten.

Lee laughed and said, "Hey screw it. Let's just go have our one drink."

As they entered the dimly lit club, Lee caught his reflection in the window and couldn't help but admire himself in his new orange jacket. He knew he looked fabulous.

They sat at the bar. Feeling totally out of it, almost sick, Duffy lay his head down – too many beers for him. Lee wasn't feeling any pain and still in high spirits, struck up a conversation with the guys sitting next to 'im on the bar stools.

"Where you guys from?" he queried.

The big guy in the leather jacket smiled. "We're from the Bay area – we're called the East Bay Boys." They chatted for awhile. The two East Bay Boys insisted on buying him another drink, and another, and another. Then, the big guy whispered, "Hey, I like you – so I'm going to let you in on a little secret. I've got some real special stuff. And I'll let you have some real cheap, below cost. Only sissies never tried it and, I'm telling you, it *is* real good."

Stumbling, Lee followed them into the small narrow side alley, thinking to himself, "Never tried any dope, but hey, why not – I'm living!"

It was all he got out before the big guy slugged him. As he went down, he heard the cry escape his already bleeding lip. "Why?"

"Did you hear that, Joe?" the big bruiser smirked. "The little queer, the faggot in the orange jacket, wants to know why?"

Hearing his words as if they were far away, Lee tried to reply. "But, I'm not..." Just then, a kick to his ribs took his breath, then the kick to his head from the big guy's buddy, Joe. That swam him into unconsciousness.

It was an honest mistake. Seeing Lee stumbling around here in the District in his beautiful orange jacket, they'd assumed he was gay. There was no way that Lee could have known that some of the East Bay

Boys were noted for their cruelties. They'd come to the Castro District to go fishing – for queers. It was one of their sports. They hated gays as much as Lee.

Lee's unconsciousness led him into coma from which he'd never return. Horrified, Duffy found him later – the orange jacket nearby, torn and covered in Lee's blood – useless.

Bad Afternoon for a Piece of Cake

He went through life looking up at people. Dapper Dan the Man, as he was called, was short at 5'2". Dan Holden didn't really mind because it gave him an advantage – he saw things other people missed. It'd helped him in business considerably. He was the CFO and a major stockholder for an international conglomerate, one of the Fortune 15 powerhouse companies with its headquarters in Denver, Colorado.

Originally, Dan hailed from Meridian, Mississippi. He was educated in a small Catholic school. Actually, there were very few Catholics in his home state. The entire high school consisted of thirty-five students; his class, only *seven* students – four boys and three girls – and they didn't get away with anything. Of the boys, one became a priest, and then changed his mind, becoming a successful writer. The other three boys, including him, all became self-made millionaires. The other two owned their own companies, while Dan was smart with his investments in stocks. One of the three girls was the first woman to obtain the high-ranking position of dean at a college in that state. The second girl became the first woman to head a car company in Mississippi and the third girl became a successful movie star. So, he guessed, the nuns had done something right.

This quarter's analyst meeting was in the Big Apple. He loved New York City. His beautiful wife, Donna, a statuesque blonde, was successful in her own right as a psychologist. They made weekend getaway trips there whenever they could – they both loved Broadway shows. But this time, like so many others, he came alone. Donna was off to Miami for the annual meeting of the American Psychological Association, where she was a board member.

He arrived for the off-site luncheon at the 21 Club a half-hour early, so he settled at the bar to enjoy a martini in the midst of the ambiance proffered by the rich mahogany wood, the uniquely exquisite lighting, all while being inspected by celebrity headshots around the bar, seemingly watching the play of life.

A petite, all-American brunette, a knockout, probably in her mid-twenties, perched herself on the barstool to his right. Real pearls. Nice touch to the lavender chenille suit that accented her hazel eyes. She placed her clutch on the bar, glanced at his martini and ordered one for herself.

Her drink arrived quickly. While she deliberately toyed with the olive between her teeth with her tongue, she took the initiative.

"Excuse me. You haven't, by any chance, seen a tall, dark, handsome gentleman sitting alone at the bar, as if he's waiting, or maybe looking for someone, have you?"

"Ahhh," for an instant Dan was a little thrown, wondering if she was talking to him. New York wasn't the friendliest of places, but because she was looking directly at him, he glanced around and politely answered, "No. Sorry. But then, I just got here myself."

She shrugged a smile at him and sighed. "Neither have I, but then, maybe one of these days, who knows!" She laughed as her eyes danced at him.

"Eh, ha, hmmm," as he coughed a nervous laugh, more with embarrassment than anything else because he wasn't sure what she was talking about.

Picking up her purse, her hand, adorned with long red fingernails, gracefully withdrew a silver case. She popped it open, lazily took out a cigarette, licked the tip, and casually held it between her very red lips. She turned to him and waited. At first he just stared at her, then realized she was waiting for a light.

Sheesh, was he thick or what? He patted his coat as if he expected matches or a lighter to appear. He never carried either because he didn't smoke. He looked for matches on the bar, finding none. He realized why. "Isn't it illegal to smoke in bars here?" he asked her. She wrapped her lips around the edge of the cigarette, and while she pretended to take a puff, she looked directly into his eyes. Then she put the cigarette back into her bag. That was really something. He had to shake himself back to reality.

Pointing at the few pictures over the bar of retired Yankees and Mets, she chattered on, making witty and interesting conversation.

"For a girl, she sure knows a lot about sports," Dan thought to himself. Knowing his cohorts would arrive at any minute, he looked at his watch.

She quickly changed the topic. "You have an appointment?"

"Uh, just a boring kinda business lunch," he chuckled.

"Well, I have to go to work." She tilted her glass taking the last sip of her drink.

"What kind of work do you do?" he inquired with no particular enthusiasm.

"Ohhh, pleasurable work," she smiled, tilted her head, and coyly continued, "Enjoyable, fun work. But, I need a partner. You interested?"

"I beg your pardon?" he gaped before he could stop himself. God, had he really said such a stupid thing, he asked himself?

"You don't have to *beg,* honey." She gave a throaty velvety laugh that was followed by a very sweet and innocent-like smile. "Just request. It's five hundred dollars for a couple of hours and it's nice. Real nice."

Dapper Dan the Man, who thought he was fairly sophisticated, was stunned. He didn't see that one coming. Dan was a faithful man.

He'd never, not once, cheated on his wife. Not in the eighteen years of their marriage, and he believed she was totally faithful as well. They'd both been raised Catholic. He loved her with all his heart. They raised their three wonderful children – sixteen-year-old Megan, fourteen-year-old Aidan and twelve-year-old Elizabeth – in the Catholic faith. They all went to Mass every Sunday and tried to lead a moral life.

But, there was, however, one *little chink* in his ego's armor. It seemed that every time they had these "business meetings," all the other guys did cheat on their wives. And they consistently made fun of him for being Mr. Goody Two Shoes, as they'd pegged him, razzing and mocking him from day one, like he was an embarrassment to them.

It had gone on for years.

He didn't want to cheat on his wife. He wasn't horny. He'd never find any sex better than with his own wife, and really didn't want to. Why take a drink of tainted water when his own pond was pure?

Well, it wasn't about sex at all. It was simply that he was so damn sick of the guys jiving him all the time. Out of the corner of his eye, he'd seen three of the guys walk in, obviously surprised that he was sitting with a dame – and he knew that, in their opinion, this dame was some good looking piece of cake – well, in his opinion too. The fellows hadn't even come up to him. They were in the corner, staring and whispering like teenagers. This was his one chance to stop 'em, once and for all. Heck, he didn't even have to go through with it – all he had to do was walk out with her.

"Let's go." He said to the young woman as he stood and threw back his shoulders. He paid the check, took her arm and waltzed her out, strutting like a Banty Rooster.

"I'll be back." He said in a low voice as he acknowledged the guys.

He had no idea what he was really going to do. They got a cab, she gave an address and they pulled up to a fairly nice building. They walked into a small foyer with a stairway in front of them.

"Follow me," she smiled and started up the stairs.

"Hey, wait, where's the elevator?"

"Oh, we don't need one," she laughed as she looked back, "because there isn't one. It's a walk-up. Not far. C'mon."

"If she can make it in those heels, I can sure do it," he thought. Five flights later, gasping for breath, he made a mental note to begin working out again. By the time they arrived at her front door, he was perspiring. No, he was by-God sweating.

She unlocked the door and ushered him inside. He stepped into an attractive living room and as he surveyed her place, he heard the clack of her lock. She was leaning against the door, smiling. She tossed her purse on the sofa and kicked off her shoes. She took three steps toward him, smiled sweetly with her hands on her hips and whispered, "Hit me!"

"I beg your pardon?" He wondered if he'd heard correctly.

"Like I said before, honey, you don't have to beg! Just do it. Do as you're told." Her voice had a firmer tone as she repeated, "Hit me!"

"Oooooooof."

His mind spun as he sucked for breath that wouldn't come, bent at the waist from an incredibly high kick to his gut. He never saw the upper cut to his chin that straightened him back up as he groaned for breath. Stepping towards her was clearly a mistake as another kick to his stomach doubled him over again. This breath thing wasn't working too well.

"What the hell, "he blurted, "Are you some kind of martial arts master?" His mind caught up to this stupid comment and he rationally moaned between his teeth, *Are you nuts?"*

She grabbed his jacket lapels with both hands just as he shoved her away, but she didn't let go. Hearing the rip of the cloth, he knew this was one strong lady because it was damn expensive and solid gabardine material.

Knocking him on the bed, she clutched his shirt, and yanked violently. He heard buttons giving up and the shirt followed suit – more skriiitchhhing of material surrendering. Having caught his breath, he rolled off the bed and mustered a standing posture, hands raised to fend off the certain blows. As she came at him yet again, he began thinking better of warding off blows and he took to running. Running around the whole apartment with the bitch – that's what ole spiritual Dan's mind was registering just now – in hot pursuit.

"You bastard, I said hit me!" she screamed.

Blood from his nose flowed freely down his chin and onto what was left of his shirt   .

"Oh, God," he rasped out loud, "I got to get out. She's going to kill me!"

It was very clear that she was one of those masochists he'd read about, but she was schizo too, because she sure as hell was acting like a sadist now. Whatever she was, there were definitely more than a few loose screws in there.

Once again, catching up to him, she grabbed at his shoulder, those red fingernails digging into his neck.

Yelling at the top of his lungs and in a complete panic, he jerked away from her with only one choice feasible. He drew back and slugged her. The shot sent her sprawling backwards, out onto the bed. He toyed only briefly with calling 911 as he leaned in to see how badly she was hurt. Moving her head, she moaned slowly, "Ohhh, yes! C'mon, baby, let's play."

Turning, he ran towards the front door, fingers desperately fumbling as he unlocked it and fled for his life.

He walked back into 21 looking like the lone survivor of a dog fight – battered and bruised, still wearing the blood-soaked and torn shirt and the jacket with the flapping lapel.

Everyone stared, but no one said a word. The whole restaurant fell silent. You could hear a pin drop as he walked to his friends' table. They simply sat there staring, mouths agape. He didn't care. Dapper Dan the Man would never again care what people thought of him as long as he lived.

He jabbed his finger at them as he spoke between gritted teeth with a quiet but ominous voice, "Don't you... any of you.... ever say anything to me about not cheating on my wife. Ever again – you hear me? Keep your traps shut!"

Turning, he walked out, as he thought to himself, "It was a bad afternoon for a piece of cake – especially one that isn't really yours to taste!"

The Battery and More

"New York, New York, it's a wonderful town,
The Bronx is up and the Battery's down,
The people ride in a hole in the ground . . ."

The early morning light backlit the girl's reflection in the windows of upper Madison Avenue. Her image was stunning. Passers-by turned their heads in hopes of catching a full-on glance of the statuesque mulatto humming her way from shop to shop. Few would have guessed her talent was as magnificent as her looks. She was mentally working her way through her repertoire for a performance later in the week – her enrollment at The Julliard School of Music belied her talent and hinted at her work ethic.

"New York, New York," Green and Comden's great song from the musical *On the Town* is one of her all-time favorites. The Battery, on the southern tip of Manhattan, was named for the artillery battery that defended the harbor even before the Revolutionary War. With a plaid history, it was now where tourists boarded ferries to the Statue of Liberty and Ellis Island. It's located down from downtown, so the Battery's "down."

Ramona had always been resolute, born of a blonde, blue-eyed, fair-skinned English mother and a father from Africa as black as coal – a unique background at the time she was born. She always felt as if she was outside looking in – the observer – maybe that was because of her heritage as a mixed race.

Her mother was a writer who, before Ramona, had been married to an older, extremely wealthy man whom she loved dearly. Together, they had two daughters. One unfortunate day while on his boat off the coast of Florida, he dove off the deck for his usual morning swim only to have death grip his heart and hold on. His body washed up on shore.

The family washed out.

Her mother inched toward making grieving a career. She refused in the ensuing years to become romantically involved with anyone. She had lost her great love.

After seven of those lonely years, she found herself busied in civic matters. She'd been teamed with an extremely handsome black gentleman, a political leader, for a rather large project. They worked well together for some time, never giving a relationship a second thought. He, having been raised in Mississippi during prejudiced times, was not about to have an affair with a white woman, English or otherwise. But one late night after an exhaustive work day, he did insist on dinner – it was the gentlemanly thing to do. Famished, she acquiesced and after a couple of glasses of wine, found herself in the most interesting and enjoyable conversation she'd had in years. There was even laughter!

He saw her home and one unexpected thing led to another. Her mother fell madly in love for the second time in her life and shortly after, she found herself with child.

She wasn't about to abort the pregnancy but she refused to marry him despite his pleas. Culturally, she realized the differences in their worlds and those of a country unprepared for what was to be. And with that, Ramona was born into this melting pot, already different than most. Some would say a cut above.

She'd been unique from the get-go. When Ramona was just four, she already had a flair for drama, flavored heavily with her humorous wit. One evening, out to dinner, she was very aware of the elderly WASPish couple at the adjoining table, staring at her fair-skinned mother and the dark, kinky-haired child. Ramona was a bit of a drama queen, even as a child. Putting the back of her hand to her forehead, she spoke in a voice loud enough for all to hear.

"Oh, Mother, my Mother... there I was, out on the street, *abandoned,* and you took me in! Oh, how good you are, Mother. My dear Mother!"

"Stop it, Ramona," hissed her mother in an angry clipped British accent. "Stop it this instant, making up stuff like that!"

That was Ramona's debut – she never stopped it, her show was continuous, and she never lost her wit and humor. She knew she was a very lucky girl, a loved child who lived in a beautiful home with plenty to eat. And Mommy provided a great education – the best schools as well as the best social opportunities. Her mother continually stressed that she *must* always help the underdog. It was because of that training and mindset that Ramona always seemed to be getting mixed up in something on the edge.

Sure enough, as she turned the corner, her antennae went up as her attention was drawn to the older foreign woman sobbing, actually wailing, in the middle of the sidewalk. Ramona had that intuitive alert in her head that repeated, "Warning." Her mind said, "Run," but her feet didn't hear.

Ramona spent an instant trying to decide if the woman was Syrian, Iranian, Italian, or what. But no matter. It only mattered to try and figure out how to help. The old lady wore a not-too-stylish long dress and dowdy shawl and was doing a very slow spin while wailing. She held something in her fists that she kept raising toward heaven.

"Ah dunno... hawoh to goh... whyat to do... pleses halp me... Oh Gawd... he's mah SAN... he's in JAL... PLESE halpa heem... Ah mus halpa mah SAN... Oh GAWD..." Tears streamed down her anguished face and as Ramona stepped past her, the old lady grabbed onto her dress, desperately clutching and pawing to get her attention.

Taken aback, Ramona tried to quiet her. "Hey, ma'am, it's okay. We'll get you some help. Calm down now."

But, the woman kept crying, the foreign chant kept coming, and no help was in sight. A very attractive, well-dressed black woman rounded the corner in a hurry and pulled up short, assessing her chances of getting past the wailing dance in front of her. Wide-eyed, she muttered, "What in God's name is going on here?"

Ramona glanced back at the welcome intruder and offered, "She's obviously distraught, crying for some kind of help. Something about her son in jail and she needs to get to him. She wants us to help her."

"What d'ya mean *us?* I don't wanta get involved in any of this mess!"

Ramona angrily spat back, "Hey, you can't just walk off and leave me alone trying to help her!"

"Halp meh pleeses, I payh yu!" the woman screamed, offering her fistfuls of one-hundred dollar bills.

"Good God," the black lady snipped as she pushed the woman's hands down. "Put that money away, right now. You want to get mugged right here before God and everybody? Jesus!"

"Well," Ramona shook her head wisely as she pulled out her cell phone. "We can't just stand here like this! I'm going to call the police and..."

"Hey, hell no! Wait just a darn minute here – you call the police, I'm gone. I'm not gonna stand around and wait for no mess!"

"Well, then. What do you suggest we do? Because we sure as heck need to do something. We can't leave her like this."

"Alright!" the woman clipped as she held up a hand in Ramona's face, looking for silence. "Let me think. Okay, listen, my car's right there. I'll drive 'er to the damn jail but I'm *not* goin' alone and I'm *not* the one who's gonna take her inside. Drivin' her will be as far as my good deed goes. Take it or leave it!"

Ramona hesitated, "Well… I…"

The lady huffed and turned to walk away. "To heck with it. You take care of her. I'm gone – enough is enough – I don't need none of *this!"*

"Wait," Ramona pled. She had this strange feeling of being "put upon" which she couldn't quite sort out. Synchronistically, at that very moment, a friend of hers from school walked by and would tell her later that he saw this strange look of panic in her eyes. He was tempted to stop to see what was going on, but it appeared to be a private situation between relatives. So he merely nodded and went on his way.

Ramona wanted to ask his help and would wonder later why she hadn't, but embarrassed, she'd let the moment pass—it was gone that fast. "Okay." Ramona took a deep breath. "Let's just do it. I mean, hey, the jail isn't too far away." She led the wailing woman to the green Impala.

"Get in," the woman commanded.

They put the old lady in the back seat and then Ramona was ushered into the car from the driver's side. As she slid over to the passenger's side, Ramona saw the handle on the door was broken, meaning that she could not get out. And the car couldn't be more than a year old.

Two bottles clinked together on the floor directly behind her seat. The old woman must've kicked them. That really unsettled her. Wiping perspiration off her brow, Ramona tried to lower the window but the button didn't work. She looked up to see they weren't headed in the direction of the jail.

"Hey, where are you going?" demanded Ramona, irritation clawing through her voice. "This isn't the way to the jail."

The woman shrugged again, answering with indifference, "I've got to make a quick stop at the Greyhound station, first."

"I don't think so." Ramona shot back firmly.

"What? Somebody left off a suitcase I've got to pick up, so don't you be tellin' me my business, bitch! I'm doin' y'all a favor here!" she snarled as she propped her elbow on her open window.

Ramona's heart was pounding, fear and anger drumming in her ears. As they abruptly stopped at a red light, Ramona noticed a police car with two patrolmen in it, cattycorner to theirs. She had never acted so fast in her life. Before you could blink she was on her knees, across the woman, as she screamed and waved one arm out the driver's window. The policemen saw her.

The woman pushed her aside, opened her door and jumped out yelling, "You get out of my car *right now!*" Ramona tumbled out and sprinted to the police car. She ran up to the driver, who was now standing by his door, and began spilling her plight. She was telling them what had happened, babbling a mile-a-minute, at least two octaves higher than usual.

One of the policemen calmed Ramona down, taking the time to get the details of what was exactly going down, while the other policeman was busy taking the Impala license down and running it. When she was finished with her story the policeman's partner joined them, saying, "Car's stolen. They'll change the plates with one of the many sets they probably have in the trunk as soon as they're a few blocks away. They'll get to a swap point and get a new car. We've seen this worked over the last few weeks. You're lucky you ran."

Ramona was taken to the police station to file a report and she got an earful from the cops, as well as another of life's lessons – pay attention to that intuitive voice, especially when it screams. It turned out that her experience wasn't the first, not even the tenth. What she'd just done probably saved her from a fate that could've been worse than death.

"That's right, Missy," said a big Irish cop with the gentle voice as he shook his head. "You're lucky. We've got seventeen young ladies, all about your age, missing. We haven't, so far, been able to find those girls. However, two got away. One down at the Greyhound station, and the other one escaped from the back roads of Louisiana of all places – but she don't know where she was! It's a racket alright, and darn well-organized. These thugs have thought this one out pretty well. Could've been pretty horrible – a total set-up."

"That's right, young lady," chimed the other cop, shaking his head angrily as well.

The big cop continued explaining. "They use an old lady as a ploy. Then the manipulator, the black lady or someone like her, moves in – supposedly accidental – but it's all timed out. Their plan, it seems, is to get you in the car and as they get near the bus station, the old lady – who's not really so old – smacks you on the head with a bottle, enough to daze you, and then gives you a shot of morphine. At least that's what we can figure based on what the two girls who got away remembered.

"Seems that the perpetrators pull up to a waiting van and transfer you for the trip south. This one young lady said they kept her doped-up during the entire trip – all the way to the backwoods of Louisiana – to some kind of a club, with gambling and girls.

"Uh huh," he sighed. "Love slaves for sale – kidnapped and doped up, so how're they going to get away? Maybe never! A horrible, hell of a life. And we're gonna by-God get 'em. But until we do, lady, don't ever, never get into a vehicle again with strangers. Please."

She went straight home instead of going to school. She couldn't.

"I'll just practice at home," she told herself. She went directly inside. Sat down, still shaking, and started immediately to sing:

*"New York, New York, it's a helluva town
The Bronx is up and the Battery's..."*

Suddenly Ramona jumped up and bolted into the bathroom... and vomited. Wiping her mouth, she sat on the cold linoleum and nodded to herself as she thought, "My God in heaven, I am a lucky girl..." Then, another thought entered her head and she smiled, "Well, if I had been kidnapped and taken down to some ole club in Louisiana, I bet I'd've been the *only singer there!*"

She was so young…

The Seven Manly Men

The Manly Men gathered around the fire, egos circling each other like wolves, each wanting companionship, needing respect, claiming himself. Coffee was sipped as only a few sighs, a small laugh, and a grunt were heard over the crackling fire as twilight crept its way to night.

They were in the King's home. Of all the actors, he was the king. Many questioned his reign, some in secret places jibed, even mocked, but the true artist knew: HE still reigned.

"In brooding silence he sits, a twinkle of amusement in his eye though seemingly sad," the Indian thought as he observed them all.

The King was like Buddha. Loneliness permeated his being from deep within – the loneliness of wisdom.

"So, who're you working with?"

It was the man on the fringe of the group. The scared one, the weak one, the hanger-on, the Remora – the fish who attaches itself to the shark for transportation and food.

The Indian knew, of course, that this actor was after the director's name, and the real unstated question was, "Are there ANY parts I could do, any bits, even? Anything… not cast?"

Words trickled forth. The Pilot, as the Irish man was called, with a self-styled title that alluded to his flying – climbing through clouds with such patriarchic roots. How ironic that this Irish pilot should be the most chauvinistic of all the men when, in fact, the Indian knew full well that

Ireland is the only country who employs even more female pilots than their male counterparts.

"How're the winds?" the King asked.

"Well," Pilot muttered, "there was a Piper Navajo over Prescott reported sporadic icing through broken clouds at 11,000 feet." He shook his head. "That doesn't worry me so much. I mean, all I have to do is just get above it, but," he glanced over at the Indian and with a pretentious friendly innuendo and laughed, "You failed in your mission to open a hole for me today."

The Indian knew it was a zinger. Last night, Pilot remarked on the rotten weather and asked if the Indian could do something. "Hey," he said, "you Indians do chants and dances to move clouds and things, right? I'm depending on you to clear up that sky before morning!"

The Indian had ignored him then, and now.

Pilot turned to the others, shifting his shoulders in a manly man's way. "I could take off. L.A.'s good. It's 2,000 broken, but well, Phoenix is obscured. I think I'll do it. Hell, I'm not afraid!"

The King hardly moved but there was a touch of disgust that flashed across his face, hardly perceptible to anyone but the Indian. He muttered almost inaudibly, "If I have to go up 3,000 feet to get to 32 degrees, well, I don't need somebody else to tell me there's gonna be icing. Then of course, I'm not a pilot. Just an actor who recognizes that if my face gets cut up, I'd just as soon be dead 'cause I'll never work again." He smiled contemplatively.

The room fell silent. The Pilot moved over to the bar, poured himself another apple cider from the wine jug and sat down quietly.

"So, who're you working with?" the Remora insisted.

The devil made him do it, as they say. Made him unveil the hidden feelings in the room by answering with only the woman's name in the whole cast and at the same time avoiding the Remora's real question. The King liked doing just that, breathing forth the perturbation, that which covered their exterior. The Indian could see inside them and knew that even when women weren't present, just the invoking of their essences could produce the same effect. The great fathers had made it so.

The King knew it also and he liked to tease them, his buddies, his comrades. Anyway, the King liked saying her name. Feeling her energy on his tongue. Tasting it.

"I'm working with… Madonna."

The Remora was disappointed that they were now speaking of females and their roles. Before he could voice his displeasure the moment was interrupted by the sub-King – the Contender, who had actually moved onto the hill across the road from the King. Both now lived behind the same iron gate, subtly emanating the mystery of power.

It was as if the Contender had known that if he moved close, real close, he could pick up the King's energy. The theory for whatever it was had succeeded. The Contender had indeed climbed into a power position with, or by a following, like the King himself. But he knew better than anyone, though they all knew, that he was, in fact, NOT now, and *never* would be the King.

"Hey," the Contender laughed, "if you're working with the Madonna, all you have to do is keep your mouth shut and let her do her thing and it will be a great scene!"

They weren't referring to the singer Madonna, but to an actress with whom they'd worked. Behind her back, they called her the Madonna because they each tried to seduce her, unsuccessfully. While there was, indeed, a compliment here to the woman, there was something else: a challenge – not just to all of them but seemingly it was to all men. The Indian felt it, and something else hidden within the statement – fear. The Indian could smell it. Fear of what?

"Hey," the Contender continued. "I worked with her. When she was pregnant with her daughter! She was incredible! Is incredible!"

The Indian knew that her daughter was now twenty, so that was more than twenty years ago.

Another man whom the Indian had met earlier but did not know – an Indian also, but of a different ancestry – Navajo, had sauntered in again. He began a chess game with the King, his close friend.

Unlike the other six men there, the Navajo was not an actor. However, he did stunt work on films to make money. It was strictly for financial gain, and he worked a lot. He listened to their conversation as he set up the rough, hand-carved chess pieces on the board.

"Kinda odd," the Contender said, "that she's become a star at our age. Well, I'm only a few years older than she. What I'm saying is, ah, kind 'a like my wife, ex-wife, I mean. She, you know, was married – had the babies and all. I'm just surprised that it's NOW she's making it! Of course, the Madonna always had IT! Still does, but, her age and all. Most of the parts are for younger women. I'm not going to play opposite anybody my age, not if I can help it! Not unless they're a damn gigantic star to help the box office. Hey…" he laughed in camaraderie disclosure, assuming that they all understood and were in agreement.

The Indian knew that the Contender had a reputation. He usually had approval to even choosing his leading ladies. He had a reputation for picking ladies with whom he could score, and he liked younger women. The odd thing was that he also had a reputation for being impotent. Perhaps it was the dope which he had already set into this very evening. Dope and booze, a dangerous combination this great talent was playing with.

The Indian wondered why in all these twenty years the Contender, if he thought the Madonna was such an outstanding talent, why hadn't he seen to it that she'd gotten a good part? She was as good as when she was younger, and they all wanted to work with younger women – made them appear more desirable. Why hadn't he worked with her again? God knows there were very few good parts.

Even for men. Talent, especially in a commercial world, needed a support system. But for women, good parts, he knew, were as rare as hen's teeth. As rare as parts for Indians. He decided to voice the very question and was just about to speak out when the seventh man, a star in his own right, wrestled himself up with much ado from his prone position on the couch, rustling the paper over his head to the side. He was originally from a theater background, then broke into the business with the help of his sister – also a star. He was amazing with his drop-dead good looks. Obviously he'd been listening –and he now spoke up.

"I've known the Madonna longer than any of you. I knew her first. I'm her oldest friend." He sat up, wrestling the paper to the floor and smiled.

Friend? The Indian questioned to himself. He'd never heard Ms. Madonna speak of him, never saw him visit the set while they were filming their movie, and had never seen her appear in a film with this actor. What?

"And," the handsome star beamed with a sort of one-upmanship, "I was in acting class with her. We dated."

Suddenly, the Navajo spoke up, directing his voice to the King. "I know who you mean, this girl the Madonna." The Indian took offense to the words, "this girl," even though this star – this very woman of whom they gossiped – might have enjoyed being referred to as a girl. He didn't like the off-handed, nonchalant commonality of the other's descriptive tone.

The Navajo continued, glancing at the King, "She won that award for that director. You know, the one who came to see you on our reservation when we were filming, came to talk to you about starring in his picture." The Navajo smiled, and smugly said, "He brought his girlfriend with him. While you were having your meetings, I screwed his girlfriend."

The King silently shrugged indifferently, a look of annoyance flickering quickly across his brow.

The Indian knew the King had decided at the very last minute not to star in that director's picture. Now, he understood why. Harsh judgments. If the director could not control his own woman, he was not respected. It was believed he could not control the elements for the picture in which the King deserved to appear. The director had been judged. His girlfriend had been judged, yet he who undermined with the deed now sat here playing. "How stupid," the Indian thought to himself. "Man, even the greatest can the lowest be."

The King did not respond, just observed.

"Wait a minute," the Contender spoke up. "I never barged her. I said she's great. I mean acting. I don't know about anything else. I never tried. She was married and... I never did, guys, hey..."

The Indian knew that he spoke words of truth, yet...

"I never screwed her." The handsome star bolted to his feet. "I never said I screwed her."

The Indian looked at him and wondered if he was, in fact, lying. Then he looked at all the men slowly, and he understood. At last, he really began to understand. Again, he looked from one to the other closely as he spoke.

"You men screw. You don't love?"

There was a moment of stunned silence before all the manly men started speaking at once. All except for the King, who himself was quite startled. Amidst varied protestations, exclamations and remarks, suddenly, the Contender shouted at the Indian, "Hey, babe, it's you who wants to have sex with her. Yeah, YOU!"

The Indian nodded calmly and said, "No. You are wrong. I do not want to fuck her." He stood up and smiled. "But I do want to love her. Oh, yes, by the honor of Mother Earth, do I want to love her. You see, I understand her struggle, her pain, her heart, even her soul. But I wouldn't try – it's not my right."

He turned and started out of the room. It wasn't that he didn't like the manly men. He felt betrayed. Then suddenly, he thought sadly, "That is why the King does not smile here with his friends. He, too, understands, too well." Stopping, he turned once more and faced the King. "I understand her soul. But, you know her soul."

Leaving, as he was climbing into his automobile, he remembered the days of childhood when his father taught him the songs of birds – the songs of power. Birds were not afraid of power. They used it to fly, to sing, to be what the universe meant them to be."

But the manly men, that's what they had called themselves, in truth, were afraid. That is what he had smelled – fear. The fear of difference, of anything that was not of himself – that which a manly man could not control.

Was that why these great men had chosen women who were silly, dumb, insipid, slanderous, even manipulative? Dolls, bought, played with, wound up, used – never to be equals. These great men with the gifts of talent and power were themselves consumed with feelings of unworthiness, threatened by any equal power that was not themselves.

He felt sad and angry at lost opportunities. The Pilot was not really Irish, only a mixture of descents. The Navajo was not a true, pure-blooded Navajo – who cared? And the King – wasn't his wisdom first and foremost needed to learn to be King of Himself?

Any unknown emotion was to be kept locked up – under thumb – unless it was being used for a scene. They all seemed to feel so guilty… about what? Were these incredibly great men as lost as they seemed?

"Oh, what man can be. And oh, what woman is," he thought. "And then what we try to turn her into…"

He knew that the Madonna would never bed him, join her loins with his, have soul's kiss, spirits blend.

"Why? Because I am an Indian?" he asked himself. "Maybe not, but regardless, I would not, could not, ever hate her for this." His mind continued to peruse the scope of possibilities, believing he was wiser than his friends, the manly men. "Anyway," he consoled himself with a smile, "the new ideology demands that Indians marry their own – breed a new race!"

Deep within he heard a whisper rise from his consciousness and yet he could not, would not hear it.

"Same game, different name. All weaknesses have fear."

One's Own Kind

The five-year-old child, sitting on the floor, captured in a realm where only children of her age can dwell, curled her legs sideways, shifting her body into an invented position. Tossing her long red hair in frustration, she grabbed the broken head of her favorite doll and spitting on it, tried once more in vain to make it stick onto the sadly moistened paper body. "Get on there," she yelled out loud, "Get on there, you 'son uva bitch'."

Mary almost dropped the iron pot into which she was preparing the night's dinner of fresh peas and okra. Reacting with shock, she grabbed the little girl and shook her, exclaiming, "Moment, don't you *ever* let me hear you say that again, do you hear me!"

"But... But, I heard Daddy say it," said the frightened child, her black eyes instantly brimming with tears.

"I don't care, young lady, what you hear your daddy say. That's a bad word and he shouldn't say it and I will not have it come out of your pretty mouth one more time or I'll punish you good!"

The child thought to herself, "Boy howdy, Mama's angry." She was fearful that she might even get a spanking, which would be highly unusual, but it was just at that moment a man was screaming over the radio.

War has been declared! We are now at war... WAR!

The child'd never heard such lousy screaming. Looking back over at her Mother, she saw that her expression had changed from outraged hurt to the saddest look she'd ever seen on her mamma's face. All that yelling, and Moment had never heard that word before – *war* – what a funny word.

"Mother dear, what is war?"

"Well, honey," Mary replied quietly, "it's something very bad that grown-up people do that they shouldn't, but someday you'll understand."

Thoughts like birds on the wing brushed their tips across her curious mind. "Grown-ups slay me. What's the use of growing up when all these things they understand only tends to make 'em sad? Seems to me I'm having more fun, so why grow up?" she thought.

Actually, like most children, she was quite anxious to grow up because she was mighty inquisitive about a lot of things. Little Moment figured that if she was grown-up, she did not have to eat spinach or broccoli and instead could eat all the candy and stay up as late as she wanted and everything. AND, if being grown-up and understanding everything made you sad, "Well, heck, I'll just grow up and not unnerstan' nothin," she sighed to herself.

One man, Adolf Hitler, allowed by millions to have his way, on September 1, 1939, invaded Poland. It was a small country trapped between two feuding giants: Germany and Russia. Poland was usurped along with many others, including, "countries along the Baltic Seas such as Estonia, Latvia and Lithuania where Little People of the World who love freedom, are trampled upon when small nations are forgotten."[1]

The United States did not join in the fight for peace until it was bombed at Pearl Harbor on December 7, 1941. America entered fully with a Declaration into the Second World War.

By the time this abomination came to an end, all of Europe was

---

1   Anonymous

embarked upon a reconstruction period. Some of the prisoners, the survivors, would be returned to their countries of exile, transported in boxcars, with temperatures that dropped below 13 degrees. Bodies frozen in the night were simply shoved off the moving vehicle into the snowy bosom of a strange land, their bones to be discovered in the spring.

By the end of World War II, six million Jews would have been murdered, primarily because of their spiritual beliefs, the veneration of their own traditions and the desire to pass them intact from one generation to the next. Because the ways of the Jews were disapproved of, their businesses and means of income were confiscated. Homes and possessions were taken from them. Some were loaded into freight cars like cattle and put into concentration camps. They were beaten, tortured and raped, experimented on medically like guinea pigs, dehumanized, and *WORSE*. Their life breath was taken from them.

The Nazis – the German political party – and soldiers responsible for their country's horrors during WWII, walked these human beings into silent concrete cells. There, screams couldn't penetrate to the outside world as crude gas and acid poured in on them, painfully and horribly burning flesh as it terrifyingly extracted all possibilities of life. What should be a reminder of these horrors for generations to come have been seen by few: the remnants of the last moments of their desperate struggle, frozen forever in time by bloody marks, frantically clawed, the struggle imprinted forever on the cement walls. Their bodies were heaped like rubbish into indecent piles, while those still living, including sometimes the very children of the victims, were forced by their captors to extract the gold from the teeth of the corpses. The skin of human flesh to be used as souvenirs, such as lampshades. It is estimated that nearly three million Jews were slaughtered in this manner.

By the end of this horror, two million Catholics and thousands upon thousands of Protestants would also be murdered for their beliefs.

Altogether, twenty million Russians would be killed, including those who died in the perpetration of insane atrocities. For example, the "Murderous Van," a large boxcar-like body mounted on a motor truck, lined inside with metal and hermetically sealed, used for wholesale slaughter. Victims were stacked inside like cordwood, after which the motor's fumes were injected through a hose between the exhaust and the grating on the bottom.

Poisonous liquids anointed the lips of infants.

An exhibition of corpses was put in city arcades.

In the Ukrainian capital of Kiev, 52,000 men, women, old folks, and children were tortured and killed. Near the town of Borisov, 36 women and girls were raped. Soldiers took a sixteen-year-old, L.I. Melchukova, into the forest and brutally raped her, then impaled her with bayonets to boards propped against a tree. Then they hacked off the dying girl's breasts. [2]

The Hitlerites used Soviet children as targets for shooting practice. In Voskrsenskoye, a three-year-old boy was used as a target for setting the range for their machine guns. In the city of Levow, prominently displayed were the bodies of a mother and child impaled on the same bayonet. [3]

Murdered by the most heinous and atrocious acts, akin only to the barbarous insanity of the Romans who in the first century A.D., for sport and amusement – among other vicious acts – threw human beings to lions in the infamous Coliseum.

Seventeen million other military deaths would take place, and there were in total more civilian deaths than military thanks to bombings, starvation, massive epidemics, etc. The devastation would

[2] "The Nizkor Project – The Trial of German Major War Criminals – Vol. 7" Sitting at Nuremberg, Germany, 14th February to 26th February, 1946 – Forty-Ninth Day: Thursday, 14th February, 1946 (Part 14 of 15) (http://www.nizkor.org/hwewb/imt/tgmwc/tgmwc-o7/tgmwc-07-59-14.shtml)

[3] "Embassy of the Union of Soviet Socialist Republics-Information Bulletin," January 7, 1942 (http://www.ess.uwe.ac.uk/documents/german_attrocities_ussr.htm)

be so widespread that History would never have a complete account. If the "Consciousness of Self" had turned animal into MAN, then lack of Consciousness had returned man into animal. This was the Twentieth Century on Planet Earth.

Gasoline in America was rationed; Moment's daddy, Preston, a traveling veterinarian, had trouble all during the war getting enough. His allotment was more than most because of his line of work, but still it didn't nearly cover what he required to reach the territory where he would tend the sick farm animals and sell his medicines.

"Damn tarnation and to Hell with it! Everybody has to make sacrifices in times like these," he stated with exasperation to his wife. "Mary, we got no choice but to pack-up, bag and baggage, say goodbye to hearth and home, vegetable garden and friends. Honey, we're moving ourselves over to the Alabama Coast. I've accepted a by-God steady income job as a pipe-fitter foreman at the shipyard in a place called Chickasaw."

In the years to come, Moment would look back and wonder if her first uprooting was really caused by human beings far across the sea – people she didn't even know – cells in a body, affecting other cells in a body.

Or was in fact the reason for the move to Chickasaw based on personal reasons as well? More often than not, reasons, in fact, intertwine. In everyone's lives, do causes always cross over into a combination, forming an effect?

Preston's particular personal reason had a lot to do with guilt – a need to get away – make a change. The child is far too young to understand the kind of things that guilt can make people do.

The incident, in fact, had taken place months prior. Her mother had been looking kinda unhappy all morning. Then the call came from the babysitter, who said she couldn't come because she was feeling a mite "fluish." Afterwards, Mary started wringing her hands and whispering to herself, "I'll just have to take her with me, I will."

So, she dressed the child and taking her by the hand, they went out to a strange house. Her mommy seemed different, nervous, not like her sweet mommy. Bending to Moment and giving her a quick kiss she whispered, "Be a good girl, sugah, and wait for me, right here on the front porch."

The child sat obediently on the swing that lazy afternoon. She giggled as she observed a little yellow and white kitten out in the yard, spinning and chasing its own tail. Meanwhile, she heard some talking from inside the house as it floated past her ears. It was only when the little girl suddenly realized that her mommy's voice sounded so odd – not like it should – that she moved over to listen in at the screen.

She heard a strange lady's voice. "Yes, I'm sorry. Please don't cry. I didn't even *know* he was married. He gave me a pair of stockings for Easter."

Then Moment heard her mother crying. "He didn't give me anything, not anything."

The child tiptoed across the porch and then, crawling underneath the window, lifted herself up, and peaking in, saw her Mother's face so unhappy. Then she saw the other pretty lady with the blonde hair.

That night her parents had a big argument. When the family went downstairs for dinner at the boarding house, Mary said something to Preston and suddenly he jumped up from the table, and before he could stop himself he had slapped his wife. The child screamed. All the boarding house guests were standing up, staring.

Preston went out and when he came home that night, they argued again. Her mother had been in the other room crying and her face was all swollen. Her daddy had never hit her mother before. She thought maybe...her mother might die.

"It's not right," the child thought to herself as she lay in her bed, alone in the dark room. "Daddy's bigger and stronger than Mommy.

They always say, 'Never be a bully. Never pick on anybody, 'specially somebody smaller than you.' They lied to me." Frightened, she cried. "Everybody lies. I hate all the people in the world. I want to go hold my Mommy and tell 'er please stop crying, it hurts me so. I wish they'd stop arguing. I want to run. I can't 'cause I don't know where to go. Things will get me if I go out at night alone. I'm scared. I love 'em but I'm so unhappy… "

Chickasaw, Choctaw, Cherokee, Chickawa – all Indian names. Moment's father told her that in fact, she herself was part Cherokee Indian and should be very proud of that heritage.

Chickasaw, Alabama, for a moment in time, was one of those gathering places for all kinds of people from all over. The homes were part of a housing project in a clearing in the woods – house after house alike, row after row alike, still being developed. The streets had only been graveled.

On rainy Saturdays, the roads would fill up with water and all the kids would come out and swim in it.

"It can't be germy because that water is fresh from the heavens and the dirt is by Gawd healthy," Preston told Mary. "Mississippi red clay is made from some of the very same materials our bodies are made of: magnesium, iron, and all kinds of good minerals we need. Better than the town swimming pool over at the park, which is full of chlorine," he said.

The three trusty companions, wearing old jeans and T-shirts, laughed and splashed in the road's waters. The whole neighborhood always saw them together; the Technicolor trio, as they referred to them; Moment Rose and her new best friends in Chickasaw, Joe Pat and Lorene. The threesome made quite a combination. Moment with her carrot hair glistening like fire in the sunlight and the tow-headed little boy teasing, "You got freckles on yoah... BUT, you're pretty," he giggled.

"You stop that right now, Joe Pat, or my daddy's gonna slap you." Moment flashed her black eyes with determination. The other child, Lorene, the oldest of the three, threw back her head and laughed, her white teeth flashing like pearls against her dark skin.

Joseph Patrick, with his crystal blue eyes and corn silk hair, was pretty much like his name, which happens very rarely. It seemed to Moment that most people didn't even fit their own name. She wondered, "How's a body gonna fit anythin' in the whole world when a person starts life not even fittin' their own darn name, which they ain't even responsible foah!"

She liked her own name fair to middlin', Moment Rose. The Rose, her being Catholic and all, was a Saint's name. St. Rose of Lima, Peru had been exquisitely beautiful, with long blonde hair. All the men were in love with her but she wanted to give her life to God, so she cut off all her hair so she wouldn't tempt the men. Moment said she was gonna do the same thing. Joe Pat said she'd better not. Aside from getting a spanking, if she changed her mind it'd be kinda hard to try to trap some guy if her nickname was "Baldy." But she didn't have to worry about trapping anybody cause she was gonna grow up and marry Joe Pat, even if his mamma did say he was gonna be a priest. And they talked about the twelve kids they were gonna have and already had the names picked out.

Joe Pat sighed. "I ain't gonna marry you cause you won't ever let me spend the night with you!"

"Boy, you're dirty minded," Lorene said.

"Dirty? What you talkin bout?" he asked.

"You cannot sleep in the same bed with me," Moment said. "Mamma said it ain't proper."

"Why? You scared I'm gonna bite cha?"

"Joe Pat, I ain't gonna pay you no mind." Moment shrugged.

"Well, the kids at school ain't paying you no mind either, Moment, cause you lied.

"You said Lorene is yoah sista! How can she be yoah sista if she's black as the ace of spades!"

"'Cause," Moment yelled. "She stays in the SUN all the time and I stay inside!"

"GIRLLL, go on!" Lorene snickered.

"And that's why she's colored and... "

"DON'T call me COLORED, you ole... ole... ole white cloud! You best call me a NIGGAH cause that's what I IS!"

"Good GAWD Lorene!" Joe Pat exclaimed. "People don't want to be called niggers anymore, they want to be called colored. It's more polite."

Lorene put her hand on her hip, "I ain't so sure. I just gotta think about that. I ain't made up my mind yet."

"Could you please make it up fast. I'm all mixed up!" Moment pleaded with frustration.

Joe Pat, the energetic boy, all of nine years old, had found himself a treasure – a red crawly crawfish hiding in the mud – with which he proceeded to chase the two girls right across the yard and along the incline of the huge ditch that separated the village from the woods. Defying gravity as they ran, imitating Mark Twain's classic personas, Tom Sawyer and Huck Finn, yelling, "First one falls is a rotten egg!" It was a place where parents forbid them to play, but like all children drawn by the lure of adventure, those became conveniently obliterated words of authority.

Glass and junk were at the bottom. But also at the bottom were tadpoles and frogs to trap and mysteries for kids to explore. Some of the children that year had taken ill with typhoid fever, and the doctor suspected that perhaps the virus might be festering in the stagnant waters which remained in the crevices hidden along the sides of the ditch.

The trio quickly climbed up the slope and into the woods. No matter that their clothes were wet and clinging to their healthy young bodies. They'd dry soon enough in the sweltering southern sun. They crossed over to a clearing and pulled down the small but strong green sapling trees, bending them into riding positions. With the scent of pine filling her nostrils and the breeze blowing against her face, Moment felt full of joy and free as the butterflies above her head. She loved the magnificent colors of the little creatures and she didn't believe anybody could paint as pretty as God had when he'd designed their wings. Then she remembered her school work, dutifully dismounted, and called to the others to follow.

Loping and dodging through the woods, Moment wielded her Daddy's heavy netted pole, the one which he used to catch shiners from the river. When the children caught the butterflies, according to instructions for Sister Frances' science class, they were supposed to stick a pin through the body, mostly the heart. It was difficult for Moment to be sure where the heart was in that little itty-bitty body. They had to wait for the beautiful butterflies to die before they could take them to school and sometimes it seemed to take days. She hated it. The little creatures squirmed and flitted something pitiful-like. The children suffered almost as much as the butterflies and they wanted to make it end, and fast. Finally, in desperation, Moment took this great big ole book and she'd hold the butterfly's wings back and lay the body down inside the pages, and then squash 'em fast. She never learned anything in class from those little dead bodies. And she couldn't understand for the life of 'er WHY they didn't have her bring 'em in a big jar, with holes in the top for air, so the children could learn from the miracle of *life*.

"Lorene shivered, "I wisht I could go to yoah school with you guys. I'm gonna make sure my kids can go to the school they want cause when I grows up I'm gonna marry me a white man."

Joe Pat sighed, "You bettah go up North, they'll hang you down here."

"I'm goin' up North."

"If Joe Pat becomes a priest," Moment retorted, "I might marry me a black man."

Lorene giggled, "Yoah daddy'd kill you dead, child!"

"Well, anyway I'm not gonna be a priest so come on," he urged. "We gotta get these butterflies for science."

Moment and Joe Pat had to get up very early every morning and trek almost a mile with a chaperone, along with the other kids who were enrolled at St. Mary's or other parochial schools down in Mobile, in order to catch the bus. It headed four miles into Prentes, Alabama, then they had to transfer to another bus traveling five more miles. One of the reasons Moment's mother, Mary, had agreed to move to Chickasaw was because she was originally from Mobile, Alabama – only nine miles away and she still had relatives there. Mama felt the move was synchronistic, a term she said the great psychiatrist Jung had discovered. Moment knew that her mother, Mary, was very well-educated.

The children all had to wear uniforms – white dresses with black bows. All the other little girls came home every day so neat, but Moment's mother complained, "How come my little girl returns every day looking like a little ragamuffin? Your socks sliding down in your shoes, bow unsnapped and your clean white uniform stained and spotted with dirt?"

Moment, embarrassed, had tried. She had. But anyway, St. Mary Frances was always telling 'em, *God says we are dirt... and unto dust thou shalt return.*

"Well," Moment thought to herself defensively. "If we're born from dirt and going back to dirt, why spend all that good time in between trying to stay clean? Geeze. If clothes aren't made to get dirty, why is there a cleaners' on every stinkin block?"

"One of the reasons my dress gets all wrinkled," Moment tried to explain, "is on account of the drum strap."

"That's just an excuse, Moment. You start now, in life, young lady, arguing for your limitations – you'll get to keep them," her mama retorted angrily.

Moment couldn't remember what the word, *limitations,* in this sense, exactly meant, but she wasn't going to ask – just let it go. Her school, St. Mary's, had a band and she played the drum – not the big giant boomer, but a smaller one you hang around the neck and beat on at the waist. There are twenty-five drum players including Joe Pat, of course, marching in ceremonies and processions. Moment loved it. The nuns said it was good discipline: Left... right... left... right... left my wife and forty-eight children... left... right...

In order to please her mother and everybody else, Moment Rose had taken it upon herself to try and have more discipline. So she decided to give up her play at lunchtime and instead, prayed for the poor souls in purgatory or those heading that way. Then she'd started talking her classmates into doing the same thing. About fifteen of them all trooped daily across the street to St. Mary's huge cathedral.

It had only been about three weeks when the principal had come into her fifth grade classroom carrying the *letter,* inquiring as to who these kids were going over to church?

Thinking they were going to get punished for something, none of them were shy about jumping up quickly and blamefully, pointing at Moment. The principal then proceeded, by way of referring to a serendipitous encounter the children had, yet not realized, and so, she read the letter:

> *Forgive me for imposing on your time, but I feel I have, with gratitude, a story that I must share with you.*
> *I am a very successful businessman, who, as of late, has been in a deep depression, with more than good cause from heaven, or so I believed. A trauma,*

due to an event of catastrophic proportion – the recent loss of my beloved wife and only child simultaneously, with one harsh and horrendously cruel stroke from fate – a tragic accident caused by an irresponsible drunken driver.

Afterwards, unable to conduct any appropriate concentration on my business affairs – did not care – I wallowed in disillusionment and self-pity. The results were disastrous, forcing me into bankruptcy and a way of life to which I was unaccustomed, lowering my integrity and moral turpitude to a level equal to the man who had taken my family; a level experienced by an unfortunate few, an elite group to which I was not proud to belong. Over time, the price which I had begun to pay became evident – for in my mind's eye I saw my soul losing this earthly battle, ultimately the thought of death became a welcomed escape.

Yesterday, I had decided, would be my day of judgment. With the sun at its pinnacle, I drove home, unaware of my surroundings, knowing what awaited me. The intensity of the moment was evident in every breath I took. The groundwork had been laid, products needed to accomplish the deed had been properly purchased, the plan a step closer to fulfillment, the hour was at hand – to kill myself.

The Universe works in mysterious ways, for the act of a small child changed everything! En route, I passed your church and as distracted as I was, for whatever reason, on that day at that moment, my eye saw what my soul wanted it to see: that while hardships come and go, the beauty of innocence is connected always to God and unrealized possibilities.

Regardless of one's religion or beliefs, the events of that moment in time, seeing a small group of what could represent the future – a handful of young students – altered my very existence. Unaware of the significance of their act, of giving up their playtime to go into the church, of their own volition, to pray for something or someone. Little did they know their prayers had been answered even though they had yet to whisper a word.

Stunned, I suddenly pulled the car over to the side to reflect, and I found myself crying. I am and always have been a strong man, but on that day, surrounded by the beauty of a world so often disregarded, I cried – for myself, my wife and my child. However, I also cried for humanity that can allow pain and anguish to flourish when there is so much beauty in the simple everyday things we take for granted. Surely, if a little child can have enough discipline to give up its own playtime to go pray for one they don't even know, surely, I, as an adult, can develop the discipline to live another day! I can, at least, try – to make a better tomorrow for those children to whom I shall be forever grateful. Those children who proved that there is a higher power and that my guardian angels had not given up on me or, who knows – perhaps the angels of my late wife and child. Thank you.

"Well, sir, good Gawd!" Moment figured she'd saved somebody's life! "Holy cow!"

For the next few weeks, faithfully, she gave up all her lunch time, every day, to go to church. But the other kids were getting bored as all get out.

"Where's more letters?" they wanted to know. They were far too young to have an inkling of the realization that an event of that magnitude, if it happens even once in a lifetime, is much like a shooting star directed by someone far wiser than themselves. They wanted to play jump rope games like "mayonnaise." So, one by one, they drifted away, until there was only Moment, alone.

Sr. Mary Frances says, "Anybody can be a saint if they want to. All they have to do is choose to *BE.*"

It was at that point ten-year-old Moment decided, right then and there, "That's what I'm going to do!"

Most of all, she wanted one of those statues of the saints to come alive and talk to her. She figured they were good and supposed to still be around somewhere on the other side of the veil to help. So why couldn't they just get with it and talk to her? She'd stare and stare at the glassy eyes to see if they moved. In fact, she loved the saints so much that she began to steal all of the holy pictures out of the church.

One day, angry that nobody would join her, she marched over to church, talking to herself all the while. "Well, all right, I'll go alone and some of those saints are just going to come down, appear and talk to me TODAY! I know it!"

As Moment opened the side door, she froze. The faint magnificent singing sounded like angels, and unlike any choir she'd ever heard. Her little heart pounded and she couldn't take another step into that church. The child discovered a lot about herself. One thing for certain, she knew that she didn't have no halo – if there was any light around her body, it was probably a yellow streak right up her back, which caused her to turn and run like all get out to join the kids back in the schoolyard to play jump, jump, jump!

Moment handed Joe Pat the butterfly net and picked up the stained book. Lorene was carrying the box of dead butterflies which by now was making both the little girls sick to their stomachs, as they headed homeward.

Moment side-glanced at her friend chewing away on 'er chewing gum. There was two things that Lorene loved. Orange drink and chewing gum. She was the thriftiest little thing. Chewed that gum for days, even weeks, until she got another piece. When her mouth got tired and she needed to take a break she'd just stick it right on the end of her nose, ear lobe, or wrist! Yessiree!

Lorene didn't live in the village. They didn't allow colored to move in. She lived about two miles away and they had once met in the park and ended up playing together. Her oldest brother Duane was fifteen and he could run up the side of a house like a darn ole beetle or something, turn around in mid-air and right back down again. Moment and Joe Pat were impressed but Lorene made her brother stop teaching 'em cause she said they were "gonna break their stinkin' necks" and she'd get blamed.

Lorene's mama, Bertha, who worked as a practical nurse at a little hospital over in Prentes, Alabama, this one night appeared, out of the blue, at the Taylor home. She'd only met Moment's mama a couple of times, but there she was all crying and shaking on account of Duane. He'd come down with a real bad cold then took on a high fever and had gone into a coma! Some neighbors who had a car had helped her rush him to the Mobile Infirmary but it was wartime and there was army, air force, and naval bases all around and the hospital was desperately overcrowded with beds all in rows, even in the halls. They told Bertha to take her son home, there was nothing they, or anybody could do – he had spinal meningitis and would be dead by morning.

Bertha'd come over to the Taylor house because she knew Mr. Taylor was a doctor. Mary kept explaining that her husband was a chicken doctor but Bertha didn't care. She said, "A doctor's a doctor!" Preston's chin was quivering and he said, "Well, by God, we ain't jus gonna sit by and let that boy die."

"Preston," Mary cried. "If the Mobile Infirmary cannot help, what…"

"You just take care of Bertha," he interrupted, with his head cocked he stubbornly. "You don't ever give up on life as long as you're in life!"

Bertha was hysterical alright, and she had reason to be. Moment heard her say, "Duane's head is bending backwards – that ole disease attacks the nerves, pulls the head towards the feet and when they touch it'll break his back!"

Preston went out and found this country doctor who worked on the boy all night.

Neighbors came in to help. You could hear Duane's agonized screams throughout the countryside until the wee hours of the morning.

"Well sir," Moment thought to herself. "My Daddy's right. You don't EVER give up."

These words were to forever lead the child forth toward her own destiny. Because Duane by-God lived, and without a mark on him.

Sometimes, Lorene would spend the night. And Mary would let Moment go play over at Lorene's house and sometimes, spend the night as well. One time, one of Lorene's playmates called Moment an "ole honky," and Lorene just about tore that girl up.

Moment liked to go over there 'cause Bertha was a lot of fun. There was always a pot of black-eyed peas, turnips, and cornbread on the old iron stove and coconut cake on the kitchen table. Bertha could drink iced tea all day long and their ice cubes had these little holes in the middle of them. Moment and Lorene would stick their fingers in the center of 'em and laugh before they chewed 'em up.

Lorene would always tell Moment, "Girl, when you grow up and a man you love wants to give you a present, TAKE IT!" She said her daddy had worked for a trucking company and they didn't have much money with five kids and all. But this one time her daddy had come home with a surprise for her mamma. A fur jacket! Bertha told 'em to take it back 'cause they needed the money. He told 'er that she'd take it or he'd give it to somebody else. And that's what he did!

Lorene said he loved her mamma and he'd not run around, but he got sooo angry and hurt that he'd gone out, got drunk, met some woman, gave her the coat, and wound up marrying her!

The funny thing is that Bertha really wanted that coat. Bertha was a very religious Catholic and she didn't really believe in divorce. That's why whenever Lorene's daddy, who'd moved over to Texas, came to visit, about once a year, she'd end up goin' to bed with 'im.

It wasn't right that Lorene couldn't go to the same darn ole school with her and Joe Pat. All because of the color of her SKIN! That was just the silliest darn thing. Moment couldn't unnerstan' it all for the life of 'er.

"Lorene is a by-God Catholic and she still can't go to my stinkin' school. She's a great basketball player and her school doesn't even have a basketball team. And we could sure use her on our team, Lordy, we need'er," Moment thought to herself, puzzled. "I know if Jesus is the kind of nice Jewish boy they say he is, he'd love to see me and Lorene and Joe Pat studyin' together!"

Sister Mary Francis had showed 'em a lot of pictures depicting the time of Christ. Now the Jesuits said that Jesus had beautiful reddish-brown hair and brilliant blue eyes and wore this yarmulke all the time, and he had these pearly teeth which showed when he laughed, which was a lot. Moment was glad because she sure liked people who laughed. That's how come she liked Lorene so much. But in all these pictures, Moment noticed that in the olden days, a lot of people in Bethlehem and thereabouts, and their next-door neighbors in Egypt, didn't exactly have real white skin or hair. Moment had decided that it was best that she didn't bother discussing those pictures with her daddy. Maybe she'd best drop it, because heck, if everybody saw the pictures they might let Lorene instead of her and Joe Pat attend St. Mary's.

Moment was a natural-born singer – everybody said so – but she couldn't read music. She wanted so much to study music. She wished she could go to Lorene's school because they had great musical instruction classes – that school had rhythm. Moment's school doesn't have anything besides the stinkin' little 'tap, tap, tap of the drumming section from which she's learned all she can, which is *nothing*. Moment and Joe Pat had offered to change schools and go to Lorene's school. Mary said simply and wisely that she couldn't do that because it wasn't a Catholic school.

But heck, that wasn't it. Those people over there at Lorene's had laughed all get out, telling her, "Child, this is a black school and we can't let you come here on account of the color of your skin!"

"My school's got the sports that Lorene wants and needs and her school has got the Rhythm and Blues that I need and want, and I'm just blue about it all. The whole thing is absolutely stinking sad," Moment thought to herself. "A total waste of years in our lives – for me and Lorene."

The two girls were allowed to play for another hour before dark and they dressed up in Mary's clothes, which she'd given them to play "ladies." All the while they discussed their hopes and dreams like children tend to do and they talked about people.

Moment talked about some neighbors who'd come there from Georgia. A Mr. and Mrs. Green with four children. Mr. Green was their step-daddy and a real stinker. Their real daddy was dead. Mr. Green was a cheaperino, too! The two older kids got 25 cents a week allowance, the middle one got 15 cents and the youngest, four-year-old Nancy, got a dime. That was a total of 75 cents a week for all four of them, and those kids had to work like dogs for it. Mr. Green didn't believe in spoiling them, no sir. Neither he nor Mrs. Green didn't ever seem to be home and little Nancy was always getting locked out and coming over saying, "Whet me in, I'm fweezin'."

"We'd let her in and sure enough she'd be freezin'. She was always asking, 'Ms. Mary, are you a ghost? 'Cause you dot gold in one of yoah toofs!'"

Moment's mother always had some kind of goody but this one day Little Nancy came over and knocked on the back screen.

"Ms. Mary, you dot any candy?"

"No, Darling, I don't today. I haven't been to the grocery store."

"Well, you dot a cookie?" the child asked. Her little eyes shining with hope.

"No, honey. I don't."

"Have you dot an orange?"

"No, darling."

"Have you dot a nana?"

"NO sugah. I'm sorry."

This time she threw her little hands on her waist and made her jaw firm, "WELL HAVE YOU DOT ANY WATER?"

Moment smiled, "She's the cutest little thing, that little Nancy. My mama was always lettin' 'er work on 'er hair and play beauty parlor operator with her cause that's what she wants to be when she grows up. She was always telling my mama how much she loved her and could she please come live with us. Boy, were we stupid! We jus didn't unnerstan about all the bad things that was happening to them!"

"Bad things?" Lorene looked at her.

Moment sighed. "Little Mary had been threatened by Mr. Green that she'd better not dare say one word or show those black and blue whelps on ... "

"BLACK AND BLUE WHELPS!" Lorene exclaimed.

"That's what I'm telling you!" Moment fixed the veil on her

Mamma's old hat as she stared back at her own reflection in the mirror. "You know how we found out?" She turned to Lorene as she continued. "This one night I woke up jus' knowin' somethin' peculiar was goin' on. I walked into the living room and there was mother in the dark. being just as nosy as all get out. I said, 'Watcha doin peepin out the window in the dark?' She whispered, 'Shhh, come heah.' I joined her and there were police cars parked outside. It seems Mrs. Green was entertaining a gentleman. Mr. Green, who was supposed to be out of town, came home and grabbed a gun and was chasin 'em and was goin to kill 'em. Mrs. Green'd called the police to stop it. While we're sittin' there lookin' out the window, her husband was ovah in the woods lookin' for her boyfriend and the police were in the house and in the woods lookin' for her husband. While everybody's lookin' for everybody, up sneaks the culprit, gets in his car, which is parked next to the police car and he high-tails it right out of there, just as pretty as you please. Boy, oh boy, don't you know that takes guts?"

"Bettah than losing 'em. Just imagine if the husband'd got a jump on 'em! Ohhweeey." Lorene snickered.

"Well, while the police were there, they found out what we didn't know!" Moment shook her head, almost knocking her mama's hat off. "Mr. Green was all the time punishin' the kids. Makin 'em get nude on the bed and beat 'em with a belt or a board!"

"Lawd gawd!" Lorene almost tripped in her oversized dress-up 'Carmen Miranda' pumps. "I shoa am glad my mama nevah got married again!"

Moment frowned in a downhearted manner. "Welfare home took 'em away from their parents. Mama called to check on 'em. Said it made 'er feel discombobulated, whatever that means."

Lorene, changing into her third outfit, looked up, perplexed. Moment's mama was always making her daughter jot down these big ole words and their meanings in a tiny little notebook to learn them.

"Yes sir, I bet it broke yoah mama's heart."

With pearls of wisdom that only children can have, as winds of thought flow unimpeded, they carry pollens of truth that seed the mind and blossom forth.

She said simply, "You know, Lorene, some parents oughta NOT be parents!"

"Ain't that the truth!"

"Moment!" her mother called from the kitchen. "It's time to wash up for dinner."

"I gotta' go home. My momma'll be waiting for me."

Lorene began to peel the extra layers of clothing. "So, Little Nancy wanted to be a beauty operator, huh?"

"Uh, huh."

"I wanted to be a beauty operator but I think now, I've changed my mind. I guess I'll be a nurse like my mama. Unless I decide to be President of the United States or something! "

Moment giggled.

"I ain't spoofing," Lorene retorted. "So don't you go gettin' discombobulated."

Moment wiped the lipstick around her mouth. The whole thing had come right out of the tube cause she'd pushed too hard. Her mother was gonna be real upset.

"Lorene, how come my mamma goes to the beauty parlor to get her hair curled and yoah mamma goes to the beauty parlor to get her hair pressed straight?"

"Child, I dunno." After a pause Lorene continued thoughtfully, "Moment, how come yoah mamma puts powder on 'er face to take the shine away and my mamma puts Vaseline on 'er face to make it shine?"

"Well, I dunno," Moment replied. Then she put her hand on her hip and turned to her little friend, "Lorene, you think growing up makes you crazy?"

Germany surrendered on May 7, 1945 – V.E. DAY, but the denouement came on September 2, 1945, when the Japanese signed their surrender documents, and WWII came to a dramatic close. And along with the new changes and reversals, gas rationing came to a halt.

On the day the treaty was signed, Preston Taylor threw his tools into Chickasaw's Mobile Bay waters and quit the shipyard.

Once again he could tend and treat animals, selling wholesale and retail, P. Taylor's Medicines for Poultry and Livestock. He was chagrined because the shipyard owners, by-God, sank to the bottom of the Bay some surplus ships with typewriters and all kinds of good stuff that could have been given to poor people who needed them. He said this was going on all over the country. Said it was being done so as not to cause economic inflation.

"Hell, how can it cause inflation for people who haven't got a damn dime to their names? Why shouldn't all this stuff be given to the people who need it, can't afford to buy anything anyhow. Damn governments are crazier than hell!"

Moment was almost eleven when they moved back to Meridian, Mississippi.

Meridian means dividing line. At first lots of sweet notes came in from Joe Pat, but they would drop away as the years passed until the time came that he entered the seminary, per his Mother's wishes, in preparation for the priesthood. That wasn't going to work out, no how. He would someday indeed be married with a couple of kids. He just wasn't meant to be with his little Moment, whose piece of hair he did keep 'fo'evah'!.

At first, Lorene and Moment had written faithfully as pen pals. Little by little, however, both mothers, with respect and caring for each other in what they believed to be necessity and parental wisdom, discouraged the girls from corresponding, instructing them that they should put their time to better use. Sooo much to do, and more explicitly, to spend time with their *own kind*! The only thing is that neither Moment nor Lorene could ever figure out, "What is one's own kind?"

Surely can't just be nationality – human beings have many times over, murdered their own countrymen. Certainly isn't just religion – people have fought and even killed each other in the name of the same religion. Without a doubt, someone isn't one's own kind just because of the color of their skin – millions have killed millions with the same color of skin. Positively can't be the same community – people gossip, back-bite, spread rumors, and have fights in the same darn ole neighborhood. Definitely can't just be money that qualifies people to be your own kind cause just as many rich people fight each other and divorce as poor people. Besides, Moment read in her school book that the seven richest people in the world had killed themselves! So, what is it and how does one figure it out – this stuff about being 'One's Own Kind'?

Well, she had a whole lifetime to do it. To figure it all out.

A Note from the Author

Thank you for reading my book. I trust you enjoyed my perspectives and my learnings from the myriad of people I've had the good fortune to meet. Each one has impacted me in some way and has shaped my view of this magnificent planet, complete with its foibles.

I'm most interested in any comments you have; you can send those to me at books@exxcell.com and please visit my website at www.DianeLadd.com. My next book of short stories, Renaissance of Things Hidden, targeted for 2013.

Thank you again. May each and every one fulfill your destiny with Joy and Love in Light Eternal.

Diane Ladd